Fishlight

a dream of childhood

Other books by Cecile Pineda include:

Face

Frieze

Love Queen of the Amazon

Fishlight

a dream of childhood

Cecile Pineda

San Antonio, Texas
2001

Fishlight: A Dream of Childhood © 2001 by Author

ISBN: 0-930324-67-6 (paperback)
ISBN: 0-930324-73-0 (hardcover)

Wings Press
627 E. Guenther
San Antonio, Texas 78210
(210) 271-7805

On-line catalogue and ordering:
www.wingspress.com

The publication of *Fishlight* was supported in part by a grant from the National Endowment for the Arts.

Cover photograph © by Kathy Vargas.

pour l'enfant prodigue

"and all that was found shall be lost,
and all that was lost shall be found."

There was a little house, just an ordinary house. It had everything inside: it had a bed, and a table, and a dryer to hang the wash out over the stove, and every time the water boiled, the shirts would wave their crazy arms, my father's long johns shook and shimmied, and my mother's white opera gloves played the piano till the fingers glowed red over the gas jets.

Inside his room you could see my father reading his book till he nodded in his chair and when he fell asleep the pages would flutter and turn over on his lap. In the kitchen you could see my mother shelling peas and getting dinner ready.

When my mother called him to supper, my father woke up with a snort. His head would snap back on his neck the way it was supposed to, and the pages of his book would stop turning over and smooth themselves flat. He would close the book with a bang and slip it in the dark place where he hid things under his easy chair, and when he stood up, the world didn't go backwards anymore. But when he went in the kitchen, his chair sucked in all the lamp light till it swelled up like my mother's bread dough, only in the kitchen, my father got so little, my mother had to tie his napkin under his chin so he could eat. He kept banging on the table with his spoon till my mother brought him his Portuguese sardines. She had to open all the tins for him, but she cut herself every time because the tins never had any keys. She was always licking the blood off her thumb.

I was small enough to get inside the house, but they didn't know which house I was inside of, the big house, or the little house.

Fishlight

The house we were born in has engraved within us the hierarchy of the various functions of inhabiting....[It] is more than an embodiment of home, it is also an embodiment of dreams....It is because our memories of former dwelling places are re-lived as daydreams that these dwelling places remain within us for all time.

– Gaston Bachelard: *Le Poetique de l'espace*

My father always believed in memories. Memories live in the places they happen, he explained to me. That's why you always have to be very careful where things happen to you.

The winter before my father had to go away, it was always snowing and it never ever stopped. My mother said it was the worst winter New York ever had. Anywhere else they would be sending out the Saint Bernards to rescue all the people that got lost in the snow the way they did in Switzerland when she was growing up.

My mother and father said when they were growing up people always got tuberculosis. They were always scared I was going to catch cold. They said I was delicate. That's why they made me wear high shoes all the time and eat my supper in bed, even on the days I had to go to school. At night when she helped me to undress, my mother told me all about Babette, her baby sister, and how she got so sick nobody could even hear her crying, and how her older sister, Blanche, kept asking for oranges, only when she got diphtheria, it was winter, and where they lived they didn't have any oranges.

My mother used to light the lamp and tuck me in, and let me sit in my pajamas looking at the picture books my father always brought me, or coloring with my crayons while she was getting supper ready. Or I played with my lotto game and matched up all the animals and birds. Sometimes if I got sick and didn't have to go to school, my mother took her special book down from where she hid it in the closet. Its cover was all shiny, like patent leather shoes, except you could see the weaving underneath. All the writing had fancy curlicues and bubbles popping everywhere and tiny spurs on it my father said were serifs. Inside were pictures of things like roots, and the cells plants have that look like little boxes, and all the hungry baby lips leaves have to help them breathe, and branches with numbers on them so you could tell where all the stems and leaves were going to pop out, and flowers like daisies and eglantines and pinks. My mother even glued an edelweiss inside and when you touched it, it felt all soft and velvety. She said it grew high up on the mountain where she climbed to pick it once. Then came the silver apples and golden pears, but I liked the plums best of all, all purple and frosty with summer bloom, and the sunlight shining through the leaves just like it did the day long ago when my mother painted them in her mother's orchard. They pushed my mother's writing way into the corner. Maybe that's why after the plums, the rest of the book was empty and my mother didn't write in it anymore.

When my mother brought me my tray with my supper on it, I had to close the book and give it back because she didn't want me getting any sticky stuff on it. She said I had to eat without spilling anything because cockroaches were always hiding in the walls, just waiting till they could jump on any stray crumb. After she put the light out, I would lie in bed shivering, worrying that maybe some tiny crumb escaped. All the spots on the wall started to jiggle, like cockroaches running everywhere, hunting for the greasy thumbprint my mother said was all they needed to live on for a year.

I lay in the dark waiting for my father to come home, listening to the cars chugging up the hill, fanning light beams across the ceiling, counting the footsteps ringing on the sidewalk, and hearing the street doors squeal open and bang shut and the scrape of garbage pails getting put out for the night. Sometimes I got out of bed so I could see way down the hill outside, but the window curtains gave off a rusty smell, and when I pushed them aside, pieces of soot scattered all over the window sill and got stuck under my fingernails. I would stand a long time by the window, watching the snowflakes flutter and swirl like moths trapped inside the street lights, but when I heard footsteps coming down the hall, I jumped into my bed and threw the covers over my head and breathed loud like people do when they're supposed to be asleep. Out of the corner of one eye, I could see the door opening, and the shadow of my father looking at me in the doorway. After a while he would tell my mother I was asleep. *Elle dort,* he would say and he would close the door softly. Underneath the blankets, I could feel my cheeks get fat because, maybe in the daytime my mother still used to call me baby names like Fifinette, or Babette, or even Cecilola, but at night, when they thought I was asleep, they called me *elle.* It made me feel grown up, almost like I didn't belong to them at all.

One time, my father caught me standing barefoot at the window sill. He said I was supposed to be asleep, it was cold and drafty in my room, and if I kept getting up like that, I might catch cold and have to stay in bed. He said if I ever tried getting up again, he was going to have to smack me.

That's when he first told me about memories. Memories live in places where they first happen to you. Some memories could stay long after you jumped inside the covers, maybe even for years and years, my hand brushing aside the window curtains for example, or the sound of my bare feet. But when you least needed to remind yourself, there came the dusty smell that warned you that a memory was about to replay itself and that's how he could always tell when I wasn't in my bed, because he could still hear the slap of lost footsteps on the floor or even the sound of a misplaced cough. He said there were no secrets, no way of hiding from him because there wasn't any kind of box, or place — not even where we lived in our big apartment house — where you could lock a memory away safely enough to make sure it wouldn't come back some time and give you away.

Where we lived, the corridors were long and twisty, and the doors on every floor had letters and numbers mixed up on them. There was a big brick courtyard way inside, where nobody could see it from the street. In the winter afternoons, old men would come in ragged coats and mashed in hats. Way down in the courtyard, you could hear their footsteps shuffle in the dust. One scratched away at an old violin; one even blew a smashed up trumpet, but most of them just sang songs about mountains, or rivers, or maybe even lakes, places they came from, or places they lost, or maybe the places lost them, and when they finished, you could hear a hush come over the courtyard. Then people slid their windows open and started throwing money out. Sometimes they wrapped the money in little bits of paper so the man down there could get it where it fell, but other times you could hear the pennies bouncing and rolling all over the ground, and he would have to stoop and bend down to look for them.

Mostly it was ladies that threw the money down — all except Madame D'Eau. Madame D'Eau just opened her window and leaned way out over her geraniums and alligator pears and called Bravo! Bravo! and clapped her hands. The singer would bow and tip his hat and he would say thank you over and over till he made sure he thanked all the ladies that threw him all the money, and then his footsteps went away and you couldn't hear them anymore because they all got sucked up in the basement corridors. Once I asked my mother where the money came from all the ladies got to throw. She said they got it because their husbands went to work same as my father did.

Summertime when the air got hot, my mother let me stay up late and look out the window. In the courtyard people opened up their windows wide. The air simmered like soup, and all the noises got mixed up inside it, all the barking of dogs and the mewling of cats and all the people saying things. When it got dark where you couldn't tell color anymore, you could see people taking off their underwear before they got in bed.

I kept wishing I could have a pet, but my mother said dogs were too much trouble because you always had to feed them and you had to take them out. My father said anyway dogs were unhappy all cooped up in the city, but I said how come if they were that unhappy, all the dogs where we lived always looked so jaunty — even Snow White, the dog who belonged to Madame D'Eau. His tail was cocked sharper than a sickle and he was just as old as she was. You could tell because her hair was all white and wispy like cotton candy, and Snow White had all white hair around his muzzle, just like Madame D'Eau. Maybe that's why she called him Snow White because everywhere else he was a black dog. Madame D'Eau was all hunched up and her thick cotton stockings were always bunched up around her ankles. Every time she took Snow White out for a walk, she used to rock from side to side. My father said she had to walk that way because her legs were bowed. Once I asked her how come her shoes always looked chewed up. She said it was because Snow White always stole them before she could get out of bed to stop him. When I went to visit her, she let me give him dog biscuits, but his teeth scared me every time. They looked just like my mother's pinking shears but Madame D'Eau said he wouldn't ever bite, except when he jumped on me and knocked me down, Madame D'Eau had to help me get up. She had two angora cats, Mouche and Meez, and sometimes when I pet them, I could make them purr.

My mother hated cats even more than dogs. She said cats were dirty. They did something nasty. She said that's why Madame D'Eau's house always smelled so bad because they were always spraying, but when my mother let me play down in the courtyard, the minute she wasn't looking all the cats came out, white cats and tabbies and ginger cats and pintos. I liked to pick them up and rub my cheeks against their fur because it felt all soft, and they liked to rub up against my leggings. I liked when they made cat noises because I got to make cat noises back. Sometimes they even stuck their tails up against the wall and made them shake and shimmy and I got to watch them spray.

My mother liked me to stay down in the courtyard because she could hear me better down there. Every time she had to tell me something, she could shout out the kitchen window. My mother always said we had very nosy neighbors, never to talk in front of anybody about 'family matters'. I couldn't tell exactly what 'family matters' were supposed to be, but when my mother opened the window and screamed "It's supper time," I could hear her very well, and so could all the neighbors.

My father always said that eating and singing makes people crazy. *El que come y canta, loco se levanta,* he used to say. But my mother couldn't talk Spanish and he wouldn't ever tell her if it's supposed to make the person singing crazy, or just the person listening. Or maybe the person gets crazy eating and singing at the same time, or maybe people get crazy watching the person trying to sing while he's eating or maybe eating while he's singing. Or maybe the people go crazy because they're all trying to eat while the person is singing. Or maybe they're trying to sing while the person keeps eating.

Every night at the dinner table, my mother always said the same things. "Sit up straight, or you know what will happen."

"What?"

But my mother just said, "eat with your mouth closed so people can't see what's inside."

"But what's inside is just the same as what's outside and everyone can see everything outside, all they have to do is look."

"Now it's not time for impertinence. Now it's time to eat your supper."

Then my mother would start humming.

"*¡El que come y canta, loco se levanta!*" my father would say.

My mother didn't like it when my father talked Spanish. She said he was making fun of her. She would go in the bathroom and shut the door. But you could hear her in there, even when she made the water run. She was screaming and screaming. I kept looking at my father, but he wouldn't say anything. He just went on eating his Portuguese sardines.

One time I asked my father how come people always had to have a mother. My father said that everyone in the world has to have a mother and father, but in former times, that wasn't always the way it was.

"Because in former times, they didn't have to have a mother?"

"No. Because sometimes people didn't know why they had a father." Because he said in former times, people didn't have any books or letters or even writing, so no one could ever really find out what they thought all the time because everything they used to think or do was buried underground, and if you had to find out what it was they thought or did the only way was to go and dig it up. For instance, how did we know that people ate? Because when you dig in certain places, you find pots and pans and dishes. But he said people just left them underground when they went away to die.

Children didn't have fathers the way they do now because in former times, people didn't always know you needed them, and that's why children had to live with their mothers, except when they got older, boys got to go hunting with their fathers and play games.

"But how could they tell they were the fathers if people didn't have to have them?"

"Because they were men," my father said. But he said even so, sometimes there were mix-ups because people didn't always know exactly when they were born, or even where they came from, and that's why sometimes they got mixed up because they really came from somewhere else, only they got brought up by people who were different from their parents. My father lowered his voice so much I almost couldn't hear.

"Everyone could have a double somewhere, everyone in the world." But just as he was going to tell me about doubles, my mother came in, and my father got quieter than a stone.

I could tell about my father but maybe my mother was someone else and not the one she said she was. My father was home, and sometimes he was somewhere else. I didn't know what the other place was like and why he had to go there all the time, but I could tell he was real because he always helped me cut my meat. I don't know why my father never said anything about his brothers and sisters in Mexico or any of my cousins. Maybe because then there would be very bad problems explaining about the doubles. Because if there could be a whole family of doubles, would they all be doubles together, or would they have to be separate? And if they were doubles together, wouldn't it have to be in the same shape house? And if it was the same, wouldn't it have to be on a different street so people didn't get mixed up? Or maybe that's why they had apartment houses like the one we lived in so you could have doubles in the same apartment, but on a different floor, except if they bumped into each other in the elevator, then everyone would get mixed up because how could they tell if they were the same doubles or different doubles? Then I started thinking how people couldn't tell if they got mixed up because everyone would look the same, only they wouldn't be the same. They might get stuck with the wrong mother, only nobody could tell, because people would think you were the one they thought you were and not the other one. Then I started thinking maybe some people already got mixed up, only they didn't even know it, or maybe sometimes they could tell, only they pretended they forgot.

Once, when my mother couldn't hear, I asked my father if someone's double had to be a girl. That's when my father told me about mummies and mummy cases. He said in former times, when people got dead, they liked to put them inside a box with turned up toes on it so the people lying down inside had plenty of room to let their feet stick up. Then they would put the box inside another box, and that box inside a great big crate. Except sometimes they would put the wrong person inside the box and sometimes now, when people dig them up, they find a man inside a mummy case with the picture of a lady on it, or they find a lady inside a mummy case with the picture of a man. My father said that is why even to this day, sometimes people are one thing on the outside and another thing on the inside, and when I got older, I would understand.

My father hardly ever said anything about any of his friends, except once he said they liked to run around in the woods where nobody could see them, and they didn't have any clothes but when I started to think about all those people running around like that, they had to hide behind tree trunks because they didn't have any clothes.

That was before Mr. Pozo came. Tuesdays my mother used to go to this place at night to make her etchings. She said they had acids there that could burn your skin off, and presses so big they rumbled just like thunder, and maybe she would take me when I didn't have any school.

The first time Mr. Pozo came, my father said I could stay up late and wear my best dress, the one with the rose appliqués on it because it was Tuesday and my mother wasn't home. When the bell rang, my father ran to open the door. A man was standing out there in the hallway. He had the same clothes as my father, and wavy hair and the same black mustache exactly like my father had. His skin was olive-colored, and he came from Mexico, same as my father did. He had two boxes, one under each arm. He had to drop them in the hall so he could put his arms clear around my father till they came out in back, and my father put his arms around Mr. Pozo. He gave Mr. Pozo a kiss and Mr. Pozo kissed my father. I never saw my father kiss my mother the way he kissed Mr. Pozo. That's when I got really scared because what if they were really doubles? My father never said what happens exactly when two doubles meet. Maybe they sink back into only one person, and then I wouldn't be able to tell anymore if it was my father or Mr. Pozo. Before that, I used to think maybe a double was only half the other double, and you couldn't have a whole double until they got together, but when Mr. Pozo kissed my father, I got scared maybe it was just the opposite: you had to make sure your double didn't find you or you might get stuck and disappear.

I kept whispering to myself: Pleasegodpleasedon't makethemgetmixeduporstucktogether so my father wouldn't disappear.

Mr. Pozo kissed me and put me on his lap. He even had the same kind of teeth, exactly like my father had, only when he said things, his mouth smelled like perfume water. My father tried saying things to me in Spanish, baby things, but I couldn't tell what he was saying because when my mother was home we always talked in French. My father talked Spanish just when Mr. Pozo came. So my father asked if I wanted to play a little song for Mr. Pozo on my mother's new piano. When my mother was home, she wouldn't even let me touch the keys, so I just seesawed my elbows quickly up and down and squeezed the pedal down. I had to stand on it hard otherwise my feet couldn't even reach. When I was finished, I curtseyed like my mother taught me to.

Mr. Pozo took the biggest box off the table. He tore the paper open. Inside was a trunk with things on it like safety pins. My father asked me if I was going to open the hasps. I didn't know what hasps were supposed to be exactly, so my father showed me how when you pushed the things like safety pins apart, the trunk would open like a book. Inside it had drawers and hangers with doll dresses on them and a baby bottle. It had a doll inside dressed in underwear, all bald and pink with rubber skin that smelled just like when I got a stomach ache and my mother used to stick the hot water bottle inside my bed. But my father said I had to thank Mr. Pozo anyway. Then he made me go to my room to put on my pajamas and get in bed because it was past my bedtime and I had to get up early because I had to go to school.

I could hear my father talking and laughing with Mr. Pozo in the living room but I couldn't tell what they were saying because my father didn't talk the same. I got out of bed because they couldn't hear me anyway and I opened Mr. Pozo's trunk. The doll was in there. It tumbled out and bounced. I gave it a big fat kick. It went bouncebouncebounce. Then I gave it another. I went kickkickkickkickkick, and I stepped on it and squooshed it like it was just a rubber ball.

The door opened. My father turned on the light. I didn't want him to know what I was doing. "Put out the light," I said. I crawled into bed and hid my face inside the covers.

Next morning I went inside the living room. Mr. Pozo was gone but a book was lying on the table. It had a leather cover, all in black, with gold writing on it. I wanted maybe to open it just a little bit to see what it had inside.

"No, you don't!" my father shouted. "You can't look at that. That's Mr. Pozo's book!"

He took the book away from me and he wouldn't let me see it. Even though he used to tell me funny stories all the time and buy me picture books, my father wouldn't ever let me see inside Mr. Pozo's book.

"Why couldn't I just look at it a little bit?"

"Because there are things in it you wouldn't understand."

"Why can't I understand?"

"Because you'll understand when you get older."

"How old will I be?"

But my father didn't know.

After that, I used to think about Mr. Pozo's book all the time but my father wouldn't tell me where it was. That's why I had to look for it myself. Maybe it was some place in his room, except my father didn't always have to go to work. Some days he only worked a little. But other times he didn't work at all. He just sat in his easy chair reading books until he used to fall asleep and sometimes he would snore so loud, he woke himself up with a jerk. I had to wait till he wasn't there and my mother was busy maybe taking a bath or fixing her legs so no one could tell if I went inside my father's room. Except sometimes when my mother was fixing her legs, my father would come home, and my mother would get mad because she had to put everything away.

Every time I pushed open the door, the closet in my father's room would squeak open, *eeeeeeee.* I could see all my father's pants hanging upside down inside and all his shoes knocked over on their sides. I didn't like looking at them all empty without my father in them, but every time I tried to push the closet shut, it wouldn't stay like that. It just kept squealing open.

One time I went inside my father's room. I looked on all the shelves and in the piles of newspapers he used to stack up against the walls. I got down on my hands and knees so I could look under my father's chair. I had to lift the skirt up to look underneath, but it was so dark under there I couldn't see anything. Even when I stuck my arm in all the way up to my shoulder, I still didn't find anything. There was just gray dust and paper clips. I didn't know what my father did with Mr. Pozo's book. Maybe he took it with him when he went to work, or maybe he gave it back to Mr. Pozo, or maybe he just took it out from under his chair to look at it and he was going to put it back when he got through.

Once I went in there when I thought my mother was busy. I didn't know she heard me. "What are you doing in here? Don't you know you're not supposed to go in your father's room?"

I told her I had to get some paper clips because I needed to make a necklace with them. She gave me a funny look. "That's the last time. Now it's time to eat." She made me go to the kitchen so I could eat my lunch.

My father didn't like time. He used to say it didn't really matter what time people ate their lunch or even dinner. He said God couldn't ever tell if things were going backwards or forwards because he never had a watch and anyway, for

him, everything was always happening at once. That's why
my father said it didn't really matter which moment came
before any other moment. He said words like before and
after were just the way people had of forgetting—because
they didn't want to remember—that, in the eye of God, everything played itself out everywhere at once.

I didn't know if maybe I was like God because I
couldn't ever tell what time it was. I always had to ask my
father but my father said God didn't have anybody he could
ask about time. I would watch him fish in his waistcoat pocket
for the gold watch on the chain he always looped through
his middle button hole. It had three lids on it that went
poppoppop, just like my mother's compact did and curly
things on back my father said were his initials. It even had
real rubies inside, only I almost never got to see them. I
always had to ask him if it was still morning or already af-
ternoon, or how soon Christmas was coming, or when it
would be Tuesday when I got to stay up late because my
mother had do her etchings and Mr. Pozo came.

I used to think for God time must be like our courtyard in summertime when the air got so sticky it forgot to
breathe, and the heat climbed higher and higher until each
floor shimmered like a mirror and you could hear people
coughing, or laughing, or crying sometimes, or saying things
in other languages, or the fat man next door drawing up
gobs of spit behind his half-closed blinds, or the boys playing hide and seek because they couldn't play hockey in the
street after it got dark. And my mother screaming and
screaming till her hair got on fire and made like it was burning up, and Alice Walsh who sang Rossini in her high, sweet
voice while she stood all soapy in the tub, and how her
brother said he'd beat me up if I told on her because even
in the tub, his sister always had clothes on when she sang,

and the parrot from the Amazon who lived somewhere downstairs and who practiced with her every morning, and when
she was done, went on hiccoughing to himself, and even the
prayers I kept whispering to God every night to make me
have blue eyes and long blond hair like they had in fairy
tales—all the sounds through the open windows of summer
when the air got too hot, too lazy to spread them very far so
they all got stuck in there long after they happened — all
those noises were not even a whisper in the courtyard of
God who had to listen to everything at once.

Once I asked my father if people ever felt sorry for
God for all the noise he had to listen to. That's when my
father looked like maybe he was smiling, or maybe it was
just because he had something that made his cheek pop
every time he closed his mouth.

"No," my father said. "Everyone who lives is writing
the history of the world." Some people were writing one
kind of history, but other people were writing something
that didn't always have to have kings or famous people in it.
He said that kind of history was called 'me-too' history because it just had ordinary people in it.

"Like Madame D'Eau?"

He said yes, even Madame D'Eau, even Snow White
was making history because whenever a dog raised a leg
over a hydrant, he was doing what even the most important
writers in the world are doing because the hydrant was the
guest book of the streets and showed messages from all the
dogs who passed by so they could read them with the moist
quiver of a nostril before adding their two cents. And God
wanted everyone to write it because he suffered from in-
somnia and he couldn't sleep because for him, all the time
was the same, and he didn't have any bed time. That's why
he always needed something to read, and people had to write

it just as fast as they could keep getting born, and it made God happy because he could hear all the noise they made at once. But even so, God didn't always have enough to read, and sometimes his mother caught him twiddling his thumbs.

"Is that why God never gets sad? Not even about the littlechildrenstarvingineurope?"

My father shook his head. "God is sadly inexperienced," he told me. "God is never hungry or thirsty because he never eats or drinks. He doesn't know what hunger means or even thirst. That's why nobody should make anyone suffer or make them cry because someday if God ever hears a person crying at a time when all the other noises in the world get still even for a minute, he might discover tears. And when God hears even one tear dropping, his heart will surely break."

"Is that why you never cry?"

"Oh," my father threw up his hands, "even if I did, who would listen?"

That's how I could tell my father was different from God because God wasn't sad yet, but my father was.

I started to think if God could hear, maybe he could see, or maybe even smell, and I wondered how come he never liked to eat or drink. Maybe it was because he could smell carrots all the time. I felt sorry for God because if he had to hear all the noises in the world at once, how could he listen to music? Or make out all the smells and all the colors in the world? To be God you had to have all gray, everything gray. After that, cloudy days always made me think of God. I asked my father how God could ever draw anything because orange and magenta wouldn't hold still long enough for him to get to see them very well, and he couldn't sing a song because all the music of a song wouldn't wait long enough for him to hear it. Even words could stop other words long enough so people could tell what they were saying, but if you were God, you couldn't ever stop long enough.

One time, I asked my father if everything had a name. I could tell he was thinking because he wrinkled his forehead the way he did when he counted words in his crossword puzzles. He said he didn't think everything in the world had to have a name. But you always needed someone to see something first before it had a name.

"What's the name of Mr. Pozo's book?"

My father made like he didn't hear. He said trees have secret places underground, especially at night when the rest of the world is sleeping, and no one, not even moles, could see them because in places where there isn't ever any light, worms and even animals couldn't even see. He said that under forests and jungles and even things as well-behaved as parks, at that very moment, mazes of roots were bumping into one another, groping for the elbows and knucklebones of other trees, sliding over and under each other in the dark, sighing and whispering, and sometimes the noise got so loud that if you put your ear to the ground, you could even hear them groaning.

He said there were places where insect armies caught slaves and kept them underground so they could milk them of this sweet stuff called honeydew and keep it hidden inside places so secret other insects would starve to death before they ever found it. Sometimes worker insects built huge towers out of dung and spit so strong that even bulldozers couldn't knock them down, and inside they locked the queen up where a secret gang of worker insects could lick this stuff off her till she got so fat and white, they had to move her into an even bigger place because she couldn't fit inside the old place anymore with all the worker insects licking all the stuff off her. But nobody could ever see how the insect workers moved her because they did it underground where nobody had eyes.

My father said the earth was like a huge chocolate, hard on the outside, but all melted like Bosco Syrup on the inside and so hot, no one could ever stand it, not even for a minute. I asked him if maybe people could eat it if it ever cooled off a little bit, but my father said it might take a million jillion years and that was too long for anyone to wait, not even for chocolate. He said there were things in the world that liked to play tricks, rocks that skittered across the floors of deserts like toy boats in a bathtub; mountains that decided to skip one day and push up in a completely different place the way I did under the covers every night, and unruly waves that ran in the wrong direction and when they smashed into other waves they raised towers of water a hundred storeys high; disobedient rivers that got sick of always running in their beds, and wound up somewhere different in the morning where they forgot their names, or who they were or even where they came from.

"Like people who get double."

My father nodded. He said there were peculiar things happening in places no one ever saw. Some things were so mysterious they sucked you down inside and you never came back out again. And there were even more mysterious things, things that he couldn't even talk about because they didn't have a name because you really couldn't see them, things like tunnels except inside them, you forgot your hands, and your knees turned to jelly. You felt like flying only you didn't have any wings. Sometimes there were things like clouds where you could roll around inside them like big pockets except there wasn't any up or down because there wasn't any gravity. He said that if gravity ever stopped, everyone would just fall up into the sky and they wouldn't be able to come down, but no one had found the switch yet that you could push to stop gravity; but if someone accidentally found the button one day, everybody might just fly off the earth and tumble in the clouds. That's why you had to be very careful not to touch anything strange-looking like a button or a switch because that's when things might happen that didn't have a name.

Sometimes on Saturdays, my father would button me up and take me down 125th Street. All along the way to the railroad station, people were strolling, showing off their satin hats and feathers. Old men in winter coats stood listening to the people playing trumpets or shiny saxophones. Sometimes if my father stopped to drop a nickel in the hat, the people would nod and just go on playing, or sometimes they would stop to say "thank you" or "God bless you," or "Hi, there, sugar," and smile at me.

When we got to Blumstein's, my father would let me stop and look inside the window to watch the people touching all the gold necklaces and rings with precious stones on them. My father said people had to have rings when they were getting married, but my father didn't have a ring.

When we got to the big train station I always made my father wait so we could see all the people hurrying inside to buy their tickets at the windows, and when the train got closer, you could feel the sidewalk rumble and shake.

The whistle shrieked so loud I could hardly hear what my father was saying. All the people came running down the stairs and you could hear their shoes clattering before you even saw them coming. You could hear the big wheels start to roll again chufchufchufchuf, faster and faster, and the whistle getting farther and farther away, and the last people tramping down the stairs and out into the sunshine.

One time, a man passed my father in the street and said 'hello', and my father said 'hello' to him and even tipped his hat.

"Who's that?" I asked my father.

But my father started pulling me by the hand because he wanted us to get to the arcade with all the flashing lights and rows of ducks and pigeons riding along on shaky little railroad tracks that made them jerk and rattle. My father would ask the man behind the counter how much for three tries and the man would say 'two bits'. My father plunked down two shiny quarters on the counter and made them spin. Then he got a wooden stool for me to stand on. The man picked a rifle out so my father could help me hold it against my purple winter coat. "Fire!" he shouted and he mashed my finger hard against the trigger. The noise was so loud I couldn't hear anything after, and the gun hit me hard in the shoulder and made me cry. My father kept taking me back there because he wanted me to get a pigeon or a duck, but I couldn't ever get anything, and the gun always hit me and the noise used to scare me and make me cry so hard sometimes I couldn't even see, and my father would have to make me dry my eyes and blow my nose.

My father used to tell me you had to be very careful the way you named some things, especially things that were wild or fierce because you never knew when they might surprise you or knock you down. He said things like that

were sometimes called catastrophes, but the gun hitting me
in the shoulder was not a catastrophe. Catastrophes were
bigger. He said catastrophes could flatten you, or turn you
into mush, or maybe roast you like a marshmallow because
they were things that could catch up with you when you
didn't even expect it, things that were fierce that you could
see most of the time, like storms, or waves. But sometimes
waves were so sneaky you couldn't even see them.

One time we went to Coney Island so my father could
teach me about waves. He carried me piggyback way out
into the ocean. There was a big wave waiting out there. It
was so big you couldn't even see it, bigger than my father
even, and it knocked him down. It started to take me away,
but my father grabbed onto me and wouldn't let me go, and
that's how I learned about catastrophe.

My father said, depending on what you called something, it might behave in ways that were stubborn or even
stupid. He said it was all because people liked to call things
namby pamby names like 'fire', or 'water', or 'wind', or even
'earth'. But things like that just bided their time and stored
up their resentment, and that's why there were earthquakes
and mud slides because mud didn't like what people were
used to calling it. It wanted to be big and important, not just
something squishy that stuck to people's boots.

I asked my father how come Mr. Pozo's book didn't
have a name.

"Whatever gave you that idea? Of course it has a
name."

He said books were just like people. "You couldn't
have people if they didn't have a name." He told me I had
seven names, but when I asked him what they were, he said
I had almost eight: Cecile and Marthe-Alice, and Victoria
and Eugenia and Trinidad. And one name was even one and

a half: Maria de las Mercedes, almost two. I asked him how he could tell which name came first, but he said with so many names, it didn't really matter which one came first. He said I was named after my mother and my grandmother on my mother's side, and my grandmother on his side and Victoria Eugenia for the queenofspain. That took care of all the names except Maria de las Mercedes which was a name and a half just because I got born on that day, but he said it was just one day, not a day and a half. He said every day had at least three names on it so people could always tell what to call their children when they were born. I asked my father how come they gave me all those extra names because I didn't even know any of my grandmothers, and I never met the queenofspain. My father said girls had to have lots of names because they needed lots of saints to watch over and protect them. Except I wasn't going to be a girl when I grew up. I was going to be a monkey, and monkeys don't need to have all those names because when you're a monkey, you don't need to have a bunch of saints watching all the time.

Another time, when I asked him, he said how an angel came to visit him.

"How could you tell if it really was an angel?"

My father laughed. "Like everything else, things have a way of announcing themselves. Take apples, for instance. Or take a pear. If it smells like an apple, it can't be a pear, and if it smells like a pear, you know it's not an apple. Same with people and same with angels. There are different kinds of people and different kinds of angels, some for one thing, others for something else, and you can tell right away because they all smell differently.

"Why are you laughing?" He raised his crooked finger the way he did sometimes when he was going to scold me. "You have to learn to see things for what they really are."

Maybe that's why he took me once to see the moon. It was so cold, the air was stiff. You could even hear the lampposts shivering. It was dark but already you could see the moonlight rising and the storm clouds racing over the roof tops. Left over hats kept turning over in the gutters, looking for the people they used to belong to.

My father had on his galoshes, the ones he liked to snap over his Cordovan leather shoes. It looked like his feet went so fast, they never even touched the ground. I had to run to keep up with him.

"Wait! Wait for me!" I was huffing and puffing, blowing steam out my mouth.

"Walk a little faster," he muttered when I caught up to him.

"Is it far?"

"It's farther."

"But I can see the moon already."

"No, you can't. Not until we get there." He took me firmly by the hand. "You can't see anything. Not yet."

The streets were empty, piled with snow. We had to walk without talking, the wind was so fierce. The bare trees swayed and shuddered in the wind. You could see lights behind all the steamy windows. You could tell from the steam how hot it was inside. Someone kept playing the violin, scraping out the same note over and over. *Eeeeeeee. Eeeeeeee.* I tried standing on tiptoe to see, but the window was steamed over and I couldn't see inside.

Way up high, a window squealed open. Something hit the sidewalk. Something hard wrapped in white paper. Maybe it was money. But when I ran to pick it up, there wasn't anything inside except a stone.

"Hurry! Hurry! You'll be late!" I looked up. Someone was leaning far out into the street, grinning and nodding, grinning and nodding. His blue eyes stared at me. But when he flipped his stocking cap aside, I could tell it was a puppet someone stuck up there. The puppet ducked inside and someone slammed the window shut.

"Where have you been?" My father caught me by the arm. "We're going to be late if you don't hurry up."

He kept pulling me up this long flight of stairs, all gray granite, with naked trees waving scary shadows on the walls.

"Do we have to go up there?"

"Just don't look up. Don't look up till we get there."

My mother was sitting on a bench. She was wearing her felt hat, the one she trimmed in black velvet. "You're late," she said. I thought maybe it was a doll, but when she said "Why can't you ever be on time?" like that, I could tell it really was my mother.

"Lie down," my mother said. I could feel her breathing on me. The bench kept going up and down, shaking under me.

"Don't rock like that," my father said. "Try to lie still."

My mother started counting, "nine, eight, seven, six..." All I could think about was my feet sticking up under the covers the time I had my tonsils out.

"Five, four, three..."

My mother was lying on the kitchen table. I could see her legs, white as marble, and her hair all rusty in the moonlight. My father kept playing the violin. Up and down. Up and down. *Eeeeeee. Eeeeeeeee.*

"Don't look," my father said. From inside my dollhouse I could see my father's skin. His arms were made of cloth and all on his back and on his belly it was cloth.

They could see inside my doll house. They could see

everything I did. I kept doing something. It was something that had a name, but I didn't know what the name of it was. My mother was whispering something to my father. She was telling him the name of what I was doing.

"It's not what you think I'm doing. I'm doing something else."

My mother and father were laughing. It was the sound black velvet makes when no one is watching. They were laughing and rocking, back and forth, back and forth, *eeeeeee, eeeeeeee*, nodding like that because they knew the name of what I was doing.

"What's the name of it?" I shouted.

But they didn't say anything. They just made a noise like black velvet. And I remember the moon with her cruel breath and my mother laughing.

My mother used to stick the hairpins in her mouth and stand in front of the mirror combing her red hair, pinning it up in the bun she used to wear whenever we went visiting. She would look in her bureau drawer till she found the right lipstick to go with what she was wearing. Sometimes she picked orange, but mostly she liked purple, or magenta. She stretched her mouth open wide and put it on, all thick and shiny. She snapped her lips closed to spread it evenly. Then she blotted them with a white tissue and dropped it in the trash. Sometimes she tweezed the hair out of her eyebrows till they looked like the feelers of a bug. She would pat at her face with the powder puff until it got all white. Then she picked up her magnifying mirror and held it up close so she could count the wrinkles all around her eyes and mouth.

She made sucking noises with her teeth. When she was done, she put everything back in the drawer and when she slid it shut, the brass pulls went clickclick.

The mirror was so high I couldn't even see in it, but one time, when she wasn't looking, I pushed the chair to where I could climb on it. I pulled open a dresser drawer with all my mother's satin underwear inside, but I stepped in very carefully so I could get on top of her dresser and reach down to get into her lipstick drawer. I got all her perfume sprayers out and her powder box with all the tiny powder puffs on it, and all the color lipsticks. They went poppop, poppop when they opened up. First I tried orange, then red, then magenta, and then this dark purple color she liked to put on when she went to make her etchings every time Mr. Pozo came. I pulled the top off her powder box, but all the powder made me sneeze and I got it over everything. I didn't hear my mother coming.

"What are you doing? Now look what a mess you made. And you ruined mother's underwear." She pulled me off the dresser and shook me by the hair. She took a big breath. "Emilio!"

When she shouted for my father to come it was because she needed him to help her give me the treatment. She made him hang onto me so I couldn't kick or hit. My mother helped him smack me every place he could. Then they dragged me down the hall around the place where the kitchen was and down past the bathroom where it got really dark. My father yanked the door open so my mother could push me out. Then they slammed it shut. Boom.

I had to stay out there for the treatment to work. I banged on the door and started to cry, but they wouldn't let me back inside. I didn't want anyone to see me crying, not our neighbor Mrs. Penfield, with her shiny brass Buddha

that she always let me touch, not even Madame D'Eau. I
didn't want them to see me with all my mother's lipstick on.
I didn't even have a hanky to blow my nose. When I wiped
it on my sweater, it made all silvery tracks along my sleeve,
but I didn't even care because they always made me stay out
there and they wouldn't let me back inside. I kept banging
and banging on the door, but they said if I kept banging like
that, they wouldn't ever let me in. They said I had to wait
till I was calmed down for the treatment to work. Then they
asked me if the treatment was working yet, and I had to say
'yes,' but they made like they didn't even hear me. "What?"
they said. I had to say it loud enough or they wouldn't let
me back inside. "Yes," I shouted very loud even though I
was still crying. My mother opened the door. She marched
me to the bathroom sink. She scrubbed my arms and all
over my face until it hurt like anything. When she got all
the lipstick off, she pushed me into my room and slammed
the door. Boom.

Outside it was already getting dark. You couldn't tell
colors anymore. Up on the roof, everything looked black,
the chimneys, the clothes lines, even the fire escape, everything like cut-outs, just the sky so dizzy green, it feels like
someone punched a hole right through it and you could
tumble clear up to that star glowing up there, all white and
cold as ice. My father said it was a planet, and it even had a
name.

Next time they put me out and slammed the door
like that, I was going to go somewhere, and when they opened
the door, I wouldn't even be there, not even if they wanted
me. I would just run away or maybe visit Madame D'Eau
and ask if maybe I could live there all the time and feed
Snow White biscuits and give her cats raw liver on Sundays
for their special treat.

I wished I could make something and maybe it wouldn't even have a name so nobody would know what it was, but it would be very big, all dizzy green with color, only I wouldn't tell anybody what it was or let anybody see it, not my mother, not my father, nobody — except maybe Madame D'Eau.

My mother came in. "I thought I said you had to go to bed. What are you doing with the window open? Close it at once and get in bed." She yanked the blankets down and slammed the door.

My mother promised to make me some dresses, but she was still mad, so she said I had to wait. Inside her room, she had all left-over stuff that people gave her, ribbons and boxes of lace, and some mint-green stuff that whispered when she ran her scissors through it and frayed in such thin wisps they floated in the air like smoke. She had all these little pieces of dresses all cut up, and ready for basting. They were lying everywhere, on the dresser, on the bed, and hanging from the headboard. And big chintz roses. She said when I learned to behave, she was going to appliqué them to all my dresses. But first, she had to write my godmother a letter.

She sat down at her big mahogany desk. I watched her slide open the tiny little doll house drawer where she kept her pens. She took out the ink bottle from the cubby hole where she kept it. She popped open the cork. It smelled just like the ether when they take your tonsils out. She dipped her pen in it and made a fat line. It was dark blue, so dark you could nearly drown in it if you looked at it too long, but it turned all coppery when my mother blew it dry.

I was scared she was going to tell my godmother what I did. "What does it say?"

She looked at me with her eel-grey eyes. "It says for her to bring me her machine."

She was making all her fancy letters on the paper, and putting in all her lacy decorations. She made little O's like bubbles, and lines tiny as ants' eyelashes, only she said watching made her too nervous to get the downstrokes straight. She said I could come back when she got ready to melt the sealing wax and I could help her squish it with her seal. It had her initials on the bottom the way they were before she got married to my father. While the wax cooled off, she bundled me up in my purple leggings and my purple riding coat. "Take this to Mayenne right now. And don't dawdle. And don't talk to anybody on the way, not even if they try to say 'hello.'"

My godmother's house was up the hill. All along the way, the snow was piled in sooty patches, choking up the gutters. You had to take a little elevator all the way up to the roof and then you had to go back down the stairs to the top floor where she lived. But sometimes people who lived on the third floor had to walk down from the roof, and other times, they had to walk up from the street. My father said some places they even had elevators that went sideways. But my godmother's house was different. And outside her door it always smelled bad because she liked to cook lungs for her cat. She didn't like to open the windows or her cat might get crazy and jump six storeys and land on a lady's head like her other cat did. When I rang the bell, she opened the door a crack. She stared at the snow melting in the dark puddle around my galoshes.

"Oh dear, you'd better not come in, you'll dirty up the rug."

She was squinting in the pale light of the landing. She was moving her lips, but she wasn't saying anything. "I can't make out anything she says."

"She says she wants the Singer. She's making me a

dress."

My mother could always go faster on my godmother's machine, only my godmother didn't like to bring it to her because she said it was too heavy. But my mother could baste all the collars and smock all the tops, and do it a lot faster with my godmother's machine. Except she said she had to concentrate and she made me go outside.

Downstairs in the courtyard I kept moping around, waiting for somebody to come out and play, but there wasn't anybody, not even a cat. I started looking inside all the corridors that went into the basement. There was this one door that was always closed, except this time someone left it open. Inside was a kind of stairway where the steps were made of iron, just like a fire escape, but if you went on tiptoe, it didn't make any noise. It went all the way, clear up to the roof, and at the top was this rusty door. It didn't have a doorknob but there was a window at the top, and if you stood on tiptoe, you could see inside. My father was cutting out long strips of newspapers with his clipping shears but my mother couldn't hear it because my father fixed the scissors so they didn't make any noise. I kept standing there on tiptoe, watching my father shut up in there cutting up his newspapers till the floor got all covered up with them. They fell everywhere like snow. Then I tiptoed back down the stairs so nobody could hear.

When my mother got through basting all the pieces, she said I could come upstairs. She took off my mittens, my snow suit, and my galoshes. She pushed the kitchen table just under her bedroom ceiling light, and she got a chair so

I could climb on top. From up there, I could see in the mirror, and every time I touched the light pull, it turned into a silvery fairy bell.

"Make yourself useful," she said. She handed me her tacking pins. Every time she told me to turn, I had to hand her a pin. I could see on top of her hair where the red color stopped. She had a little line like a street where the hair was growing white. She was talking to herself, sticking pins into my hem. "*Tourne*," she would say. "*Tourne*."

I stuck the pins between my teeth and made believe I was a fish at the bottom of the ocean with a tiny light inside my mouth. Every time she asked for a pin, I made light waves in the water.

"*Merde!*" My mother stuck her thumb. I could hear her sucking on her finger. "Why can't you pay attention?" She was waiting for me to give her another pin, but I didn't have any pins left because the fish took them all away. After that, she wouldn't let me have any more pins because she was scared I would swallow them.

Every time I turned I got to look in the mirror and touch the fairy bell and make a secret wish. I wished I had blue eyes and blond hair they way they did in fairy tales.

"When will I get beautiful?"

My mother shot me a look. "What a question! You have to suffer to be beautiful. And you won't ever be beautiful if you keep staring in the mirror all the time."

"Not even when I'm older?"

"You have beautiful hair," my mother said. She was sucking on her teeth the way she sometimes did.

She made me turn around. My father was standing in the doorway watching us. "Doesn't she look cunning in her little dress?" I didn't like it when she made her voice go up like that.

My father looked mad. "I wish you wouldn't say such stupid things. Take those silly things off her," he said, "it's late for bed." Then he went inside his room and shut the door.

I thought my mother was going to say something, but she only sucked on her teeth. She said she was too tired to sew anymore. She pulled the dress up over my head so the pins wouldn't stick my arms. .

"Get down," she said. "It's time to get undressed."

My mother was lying on her bed. Her belly was soft and white as cheese. Her chi-chis wobbled over her chest like jelly. She let me play with them. Jiggle and flop, jiggle and flop, up and down, up and down, jiggle and flop. Her nipples poked out like pink puppy noses. She was laughing and laughing and laughing so hard I could see the teeth inside her mouth. In back of them was gold.

Inside his room, my father started banging on the radiator.

"Hold still," my mother said.

"Can't you ever keep quiet?" my father shouted. "God himself couldn't concentrate with you making all that racket!"

We could hear him in there going snipsnip with his clipping shears. "Shhh. He's cutting up his newspapers again." My mother was smiling, holding a finger to her lips. She made me get up quietly so we could put everything away.

Inside his room my father kept making things. He said he
had to make things inside Mr. Pozo's book. He told me he
could show me, but they were night things, so we had to
wait till it got dark. It was in this kind of park but there
weren't any lampposts anywhere. Everything was still and
on the ground all the birds were lying on their backs, their
tiny legs all stiff, poking at the night. Everything was lined
up in straight rows, all the benches and the iron fences, and
even the trees, all in straight rows, and everything was black.
I asked him why did everything have to get black and straight
like that. He said it was because everything had to be made
out of iron, all the benches, and the fences and the trees.
He said it had to be like that because he didn't want any
color. He said color was just one of my mother's crazy ideas.

My mother used to say different things about my father. She used to call him Emilio, but every time she went
visiting, she used to call him a professor. When we were
going visiting, my mother always made me get up on the
kitchen stool. She would tell me to hold still so she could
yank and rip and pull

"Owww, it hurts."

"Come on, don't eggzajerate."

But she wouldn't stop. Rip and pull, rip and pull.
When she got done, she liked to twirl my hair around her
fingers till it came all shiny fat like sausages. Every time I
ran or skipped, they bounced up and down like the bedsprings in my father's bed.

"Why do you always have to tell people different
things about my father?"

My mother stared at me with her eel glass eyes. "Are
you pretending mother would lie?" I could hear her sucking on her teeth. She put away the comb and brush. She
made me get down from the stool so she could put my pur-

ple leggings on.

My mother used to get all nervous every time we went visiting. While we waited for the elevator, she wouldn't talk or say anything. She would just rock on one foot and then the other because it always took the elevator a long time. You could see the cage coming, all lit up through the safety glass. It would float up slowly and burp to a stop. Dan would slide the gate open very slowly so it wouldn't make any noise. He always had this cap he pulled down over his eyes so he wouldn't have to talk so much.

We got inside the elevator. My mother still didn't say where we were going. Dan slid the gate shut, clatterclatterclatter. My stomach started twisting up inside. "Where are we going?"

"I'll tell you later." She snapped her lips shut so it made all little lines around her mouth. All the way down, Dan didn't say anything. He swung open the gate, and my mother stepped into the lobby. Dan propped himself on the creaky elevator chair and shook his paper open. My mother took my hand.

"I don't want to go visiting."

She yanked me by the arm. "Come on. I'll tell you where we're going when we get outside." But outside my mother still didn't say anything. She kept sucking on her teeth.

It was cold after the last snow. We made our way between the cars and along the sidewalks. There were pieces of rock salt everywhere and you could hear it crunch every time you stepped on it. We passed by this place that had a heavy wall along it made of stone. If you climbed up and leaned over, you could see all the children down in the park throwing snow balls and playing in the snow.

"Get off," my mother said. "We're late." My mother

didn't like me climbing on my stomach because it scratched my buttons up.

"Where are we going?"

"I'll tell you when we get there."

We got to this place down some stairs that had all white ladies' heads done up with curly purple hair, with white swans and big silver letters in the window that had little silver bells.

"What does it say?"

"'Merry Christmas'"

"Did it get Christmas yet?"

But my mother said it wasn't.

I let go her hand. "I don't want to go down there."

"Come on, don't make a fuss. It's just a beauty parlor. Don't you want to be beautiful?" She took me firmly by the arm, but I couldn't go down fast because my legs were short.

My mother called the lady inside Helen. She had on white shoes with thick soles on them like platforms. She said they were nursing shoes. They squeaked on the floor every time she walked. She was sweeping piles of hair up into a gray heap. Her push broom had bright red bristles on it. My mother took off my coat and hung it up.

"I don't want her to cut my hair."

"Oh, Helen's not going to hurt you, she's just going to trim it a little bit," my mother said. She was whispering something to Helen.

Helen pumped me up on a high chair where I could see into the mirror but she turned my chair around so I couldn't see any more. The scissors went whispering outside my ears snipsnip, snipsnip. I could feel all my shiny curls sinking off my shoulders. When Helen got done, she spun my chair back around. I could see her looking at my mother in the mirror. "Doesn't she look precious in that cute little bob. Now doesn't that look nice? Aw, don't cry, honey. See how nice you look?"

But it didn't look nice. It looked like some boy was staring out at me.

"It will grow back," my mother promised, "just the way it was before." She smiled at Helen the way she did sometimes when she got embarrassed. Helen helped me down. I was squatting on the floor, trying to make all my hair go back on like my mother said it would.

"Would you like me to put that in a bag?" Helen asked, "so you could take it home?"

"That won't be necessary," my mother said. She pulled me to my feet. "Come on," she said. "We're going visiting. Maybe if you stop making such a fuss, I'll get you something nice."

My mother had this friend she used to call Aunt Gertrude, but she wasn't a real aunt, and she had to use crutches so she could walk. Once I asked my mother why she always had to walk that way. My mother said she was a psychologist. She even had something my mother said was a walker so she could go one step at a time. She had to slide her other foot to make it catch up with the front one the way I had to go downstairs because my legs were short.

My mother took me by the hand. "We're going to visit Aunt Gertrude."

"I don't want to go visiting. Could we please go home?"

"It's not visiting exactly. We have to go to Horace Mann."

Horace Mann was an old brick school with windows way up high. It had a roof with greenish stuff on it my mother said was copper. It was so steep, when the snow melted it made the longest icicles.

"Could we break an icicle off so I could suck on it?"

But my mother said there wasn't any time for icicles because Gertrude was waiting for us and we had to go inside.

We went down a long wooden corridor where we made the floor planks squeak. Inside this room they had wooden chairs with paddles on them that people used to write on, and down in front they had a long table with a shiny black top on it. There were things on the wall in front my mother said were blackboards, except they were green, and they even had brass pulls on them like my mother's dresser did. My mother said they were for sliding the boards up and down so people could reach on them to write things.

"What kind of things?"

"Things with chalk," my mother said. But then she shushed me and made me sit down because Gertrude came through this little door they had on the side. I could tell it was her because she had the walker she used to walk with. She told my mother to stand up and come down the stairs with me.

When we got down in front, I didn't know what my mother was going to do, but Gertrude made her lift me up on the shiny black top so everyone could see. They were all looking at me. They laughed at something Gertrude said. Then she made my mother take off all my clothes, and while my mother was undressing me, Gertrude kept saying things like 'child' and 'normal' and pointing at me. I didn't want all the people to see me crying because I didn't have any clothes on and my hair was all cut off but my mother made me stand me up and Gertrude kept lifting my arms up and pointing to my knees and elbows, and saying things, and all the people kept looking and writing things on the paddles they had on the chairs for them to write on. Gertrude said my mother could put my clothes back on and everybody laughed. Maybe it was something Gertrude said, or maybe my mother tugging my underpants back on because I was crying so hard she got mixed up and put them on backwards.

After that, every time my mother wanted us to go visiting, I would start to cry and when we got inside the elevator, I would lose my breakfast, and Dan would get mad because he didn't want to clean it up, so my mother couldn't take me visiting anymore.

I liked it when my father took me out. He used to take me to the park with him to the place where the wind piled up all the dead leaves and he even let me kick them up and shuffle around in them and pretend it was a hurricane. Snow covered the ground in sooty patches and the trees were all bare. Way up high a leaf kept waving over my head, but my father said it couldn't be a leaf because all the leaves had fallen down. He said it was probably a chrysalis. He said a chrysalis was exactly like a mummy case only smaller because inside a caterpillar was asleep, except in the spring, when the air got hot, a butterfly would come out and lay her eggs, and that's where baby caterpillars came from.

He made me climb up on a bench so he could lift me high up on his shoulders. It was scary up there, but he held on tight to my leggings so I wouldn't wobble or fall. He told me to break off the branch where the chrysalis was hanging.

"Did you get it?" he called up to me. The branch snapped off in my hand.

"Let me down," I said.

My father caught me in his arms. I showed him the

chrysalis. He said we should take it home and put it in a box so we could start a butterfly collection. I wanted him to take me home right away so we could put the chrysalis inside a box in case the butterfly came out, but he said the butterfly couldn't come out till the air got hot. He said first we had to go to this place where there were all the whispering people.

"What are they whispering for?"

"They're getting ready to watch the moon swallow up the sun." He explained how the moon was going to hide the sun till you couldn't even see it.

"But where will the sun go?"

"Behind the moon," my father said. He took an envelope out of his pocket, the kind people have to lick when they send a letter. He gave me this tiny piece of celluloid. It had a kind of shadow picture on it, but my father said not to look at it. He said it was just a negative to look through so you wouldn't have to look directly at the sun. He said people could get blind from looking at the sun too much. He made me hold it up close like all the whispering people did. I could see the sun glowing like a pearly thing. Then something dark started spilling over it, and it got darker and darker and all the color disappeared and when it was almost night-dark, my father said to give him back the negative so he could put it back inside the envelope. Everyone stopped whispering and even the birds got quiet. The air shivered and you could hear the ice groaning in the river.

"What happened? Where did all the color go?"

But my father didn't answer because he wasn't even there. There was just the twig lying where I left it, with the chrysalis hanging on. I was looking for my father in the dark, running everywhere holding onto the twig with the chrysalis on it. I didn't want all the whispering people to see me crying because they wanted to help me but I just made like they weren't even there. But then my father came back again. I told him why did he have to go away and leave me like that.

"Like what?"

"Like when you went away."

My father laughed. "I had to watch to see what you would do."

"But why couldn't you just watch some place where I could see?"

"Because if you could see me, how could I tell what you're going to do if I disappear?"

After that, I kept dreaming I was climbing up pink marble steps, holding my father's hand and talking to him and asking him things, and there were these trouser legs all around us walking up the stairs, but my father didn't answer because he wasn't there. There were just all these trouser legs going up the stairs.

When it was snowing, my father wouldn't take me out. He liked to sit in his easy chair reading books, but if I came to see what he was doing, he would grab my stomach and make this noise like a rubber sponge to make me go away. Sometimes he would let me look in the big dictionary lying on his lap with the little tiny pictures of emus and dodo birds, and all the animals that got extinct. One time I even asked him if Mr. Pozo's book had animals inside, but he just said things like emus and dodos got extinct because they lacked any beauty and suppleness of form and if we wanted, we could see all the creatures after they got extinct if we went to the museum.

"But if they got extinct, how come they're in the museum?"

"Because when people find their bones, they go and put them there."

To get to the museum, we had to go all the way past Amsterdam to the new subway on 125th Street, but the train was so crowded there wasn't any place to sit. We had to hang on to the handles they had on the backs of all the seats. People were sitting facing other people, but they didn't look at them. I was looking at them, only they didn't look at me either. The train shook and screamed but the tunnel was dark except for the blue lights they had for the conductor to tell when a station was coming up. They had light inside the train, only when it had to go around a bend and all the lights went out, everybody pretended nothing was happening. Sometimes you could see people holding lanterns standing outside in the tunnel as the train went by. I asked my father why they had all the lanterns. My father said so they could see in the dark because they had to fix the tracks. He had to bend down and shout so I could hear him, but when the train stopped and it got quiet, all the people stared at him.

When we got to the museum, my father held my hand so I could climb up all the stairs the way grown ups are supposed to, first one foot and then the other. We went all the way up to a big room where they had skeletons my father said were dinosaurs. He said they lived a million years ago and they laid big lizards' eggs and they ate each other up whenever they got hungry which is why none of them got left. After that we went down a little corridor that had big rocks in glass cases. Someone smashed them open so you could see the precious stones inside. My father had to lift me up so I could press a little button that made the rocks light up in the dark all bright red and blue and green and yellow. I could tell it was magic, but my father said no because the rocks had things inside called atoms that made them get excited. Then we went down another corridor with glass cases all along with butterflies inside. They were all in little boxes on top of hospital cotton, the kind my mother used to put between her toes. I felt sad for them because they had pins stuck in them so they couldn't ever fly, but my father said people liked them that way because then they could collect them, and anyway they were dead. He said when the air got hot and my chrysalis hatched, he would make a little box for it, but I told my father what if my butterfly didn't like being dead, maybe she liked flying better.

One Tuesday when Mr. Pozo came, my father said it was much too late for me to stay up, except I said it was the same time Mr. Pozo came every Tuesday and why couldn't I stay up because my mother was gone making her etchings. He said it didn't make any difference. I had to go to bed.

I could hear them in the living room laughing and talking, except I couldn't tell what they were saying because they were saying things in Spanish and I couldn't understand. I tiptoed out of bed and put my slippers on, the soft ones that didn't make any noise. I opened my door very quietly and stepped into the hall. Creakcreak. The bad part was the floor boards. You had to step on the ones that didn't make any noise. Way down the corridor, I could hear them laughing in the living room. I took one step and then another. And another. I was almost there when creakcreak went the floor. But just then Mr. Pozzo said something that made my father laugh.

From the doorway I could see them sitting on the couch, facing my mother's mirror. They were turning over the pages of a book, laughing and talking. I could tell: it was Mr. Pozo's book. Just then my father slapped the book shut. Mr. Pozo looked very surprised. I don't know how my father could tell I was standing in the doorway, but maybe the corridor wasn't dark enough. He stood up and came to the door. "What are you doing there? Aren't you supposed to be in bed?"

"I need a glass of water."

"Say 'goodnight' to Mr. Pozo." He let me peek in the doorway.

"*Buenas noches*," I said. Mr. Pozo blew me a kiss.

My father took me to the kitchen to get a glass of water, but I really wasn't thirsty and I had to pretend to drink. Then he took me to my room. After the door was closed, I could still hear them in the living room. They were talking very quietly. And then I heard them laugh.

I didn't know why the next morning the kitchen smelled so bad. I kept trying to eat my breakfast but it wouldn't go down.

"Try to eat," my mother said. She was bending down wiping something up. She said how my father got the linoleum all sticky but my father told her how he received the gift of prophecy because when he opened up the ice box in the night, he could tell ahead of time the malt bottle would fall out, but my mother said how come if he knew so much, he opened the door anyway, but my father only said he didn't have time to wipe it up just then because before he could get to be a full-fledged prophet, he had to go to his room and practice.

He kept practicing in the kitchen every night after I went to bed. He would open the refrigerator, trying to get things to fall out. Sometimes he got so mad, he called the bottles names, but they still wouldn't fall out. One night this big whoop came out of the kitchen, and I heard my mother running down the hall. I got up and tiptoed to the door to see. My father was standing by a pool of broken eggs and my mother was squatting down, spooning up all the egg puddles around him, but my father told her please to stop because he had to concentrate. That day we had omelets for breakfast, omelets for lunch and scrambled eggs for dinner. But my mouth wouldn't open up all the way it was supposed to because all those eggs made me think of dinosaurs. How could you eat anything that smelled like lizards' eggs?

When my mouth got stuck, my mother had this game she liked to play. She would go, "One spoon for mother . . . one for father . . . one for allthelittlechildrenstarvingineurope." If I spilled, she would just scoop it up and put it back inside my mouth. Sometimes, if I choked, she would have to stop except my mother didn't like to stop for anything. She even tried mixing my carrots in together with my mashed potatoes, but I didn't want to eat no matter how hard she tried to make me. Once while she was trying to coax me to eat, my father came into the kitchen with some newspaper he cut up. It had pictures of children standing in lines, all bundled up in coats and scarves and woolen mittens.

"Why are they standing in line like that?"

"They're waiting for the train to take them where it's safer."

"Please, Emilio," my mother said, "don't distract her while she's trying to eat. . . ."

"How come they have to go where it's safer?"

"Emilio . . . please. She was eating so nicely."

"Because they're bombing England."

"Emilio . . . PLEASE," my mother said.

"Who is?"

"The Germans. . . ."

"*Merde et merde et merde et MERDE!*" My mother stood up. She was getting mad.

"You'll see." My father laughed. He shook a warning finger at my mother. "Perfidious Albion will gnash her teeth, Empire will rend her garments. . . ."

My mother sat down again. "I don't think it's funny, just when she was eating so nicely. . . ."

But I wasn't eating nicely because my mouth wouldn't open, and anyway my father wasn't paying attention. He just said how every night he was reading Nostradamus to learn how to tell the future. He even started to practice all the words he didn't know. "*Pempotan, pempotan,*" he would mutter over and over as he walked up and down the corridor, laughing his sawdust laugh like the mummies did it in the House of Wax. Sometimes in the night, I could hear him hiccoughing just like the parrot did. Sometimes he would come to supper and not say anything, or he would look at the ceiling and talk in French the way Nostradamus did. "*N'en plus qu'Angleterre mangera poussiere . . .*" and he would laugh his sawdust laugh.

I asked my mother why he sometimes laughed like that.

"Shhhh. Just eat. He's worse than a somnambulist." She said prophets were like people that walk in their sleep. I asked her how come my father's eyes were always open. But she said he was in a state of prophecy and that if you made people like that wake up, they could drown.

My father kept trying to get the milk bottle to smash, and even the apple juice. One time he even got the honey jar to smash with all the honey in it. My mother said she couldn't pay the bills and we had to eat by candle light and if there were any more sticky prophecies like that she would have to go to work. My father kept swallowing. He said prophecy was not just parlor tricks. He got up from his chair. He said from now on he was going to practice prophecy over water the way Nostradamus did because divination over water was a foolproof way and besides water was much cheaper, but he didn't tell my mother how he would make all her basins disappear. Sometimes she caught him carrying them filled with water all the way from the kitchen to his room. The corridor was dark, but even when she yelled at him, he didn't spill a drop. He went right on walking because he said if ever a trace of water darkened the floor, he would have to start all over again. Once water was drawn, its surface must be left strictly undisturbed otherwise divination could never successfully take place.

My mother kept telling me how everything that happened was my father's fault. It was his fault that she couldn't pay the bills and it was his fault that we only had potatoes and carrots to eat. If only he could be a success like other husbands were, except he was always making excuses that people in his family were busy doing important things; they never had time for silly things like self-improvement. She told me her family could always pay the bills because they came from a distinguished line of alchemists and one of them even invented something she said was called flow giston. She said it was something that could make things catch fire for no apparent reason.

When I told my father what she said, he just laughed and laughed. He said flow giston couldn't even set a match on fire. It was just a myth that had to be pooh-poohed. He said how he looked down on alchemists and what a sorry lot they were. He pointed to the picture of James Watt he had hanging over his bed. "Now Watt. There was a man who opened up the floodgates of progress." He said James Watt invented the steam engine and steam was the sign of progress, and progress was a good thing. He even showed me how a kettle makes steam and how you know it's boiling from the steam because it makes it whistle and that way you could always tell if it was making progress.

He explained that before James Watt, everybody lived in a state of hopeless ignorance. People were so backward they had cars that wouldn't even run unless they were pulled along by horses, and every time they had to take a bath, or even drink a glass of water, first they had to pump it from a well. He started showing me other inventions. He had this book with things inside he said were trusses. Some you were supposed to strap on and some had laces on them, but others had things on them that looked like hasps. There was a kind of shirt that had very long sleeves with no holes in it for hands. I asked him what it was for; he said it was something to put unruly people in when they misbehaved, and if I kept trying to see Mr. Pozo's book all the time, he would have to send me where they put all the unruly people in the shirts that didn't have any hands.

My father started copying all the inventions on a kind of paper you could see through. He drew an invention that was supposed to tie people's hands to the bedposts while they were asleep. I asked him why did they want to tie their hands up like that. He said to keep the id in check. I didn't know what the id was exactly, but he said it was to cure bad habits. My mother was cleaning house and when he showed it to her, she pushed him aside. "Not in front of the child," she said. She was moving things around, sweeping behind the furniture where all the spiders had their webs. All the homeless spiders kept spinning around in circles. My father said to stop sweeping like that because all that sweeping made them crazy and they didn't have anywhere else to go, but my mother didn't pay any attention. Every time she found some money behind the furniture, she bent down to pick it up. She stuck it inside her apron pocket. When she got finished sweeping, she made my father put on his rubber galoshes that went snapsnap like slingshots so he could go out to the grocery store. When he got back, he had a big bag of potatoes he got for twenty-five cents. My mother boiled them for dinner because she still had gas to cook with. I really liked them because there weren't any carrots in them and we got to eat all of them by candlelight.

Every night before dinner my father put this red velvet cloth down on the kitchen table to show off his inventions, but my mother got all peeved because he wouldn't go to work. She told him to quit acting like his feet were in the clouds. He explained that he was through with trusses anyway because he was ready to branch out. He said he already had designs for collars and leashes to put on vicious dogs, and muzzles for their nasty snouts. He was even designing a dog guillotine. He said it was going to operate with such speed and efficiency that as the dog's head got chopped off and fell into the basket, it would still be barking and snarling and baring its teeth, entirely unaware that its former body was already in dog paradise.

I didn't want Snow White to go to paradise. My head went all hot and cold and I could feel my stomach turning upside down. I could tell I was going to be sick. My mother told my father he had to be more careful what he said next time if he didn't want to clean up the mess, especially at the dinner table when we were eating supper. But my father didn't listen. He said he had to make his first working model.

He locked himself up in his room and told my mother he didn't want to be disturbed.

I wished my mother never had to go to work. The first time she went she had to leave me all by myself because my father didn't come home. "Stay in your bed," she said, "and remember, don't get up until your father comes, and don't answer the door if anybody rings."

I got in my bed and curled up under the covers. I waited and waited. It got really dark. The street lamps went on, but still my father didn't come. I must have gotten asleep because when I woke up I heard the doorbell ringing. I didn't know who it was. I kept remembering what my mother said, but what if it was my father coming home and he forgot the key? I got up to open the door. There was Madame D'Eau. When she found out I was all alone, she got all excited. "*Mais ce n'est pas possible! Ils t'ont laisée toute seule! Viens tout de suite!*"

She helped me on with my shoes. Then we went to her apartment. Snow White jumped all over me and licked my face the way he always did. Madame D'Eau gave me a biscuit to feed him, but every time I wanted to give it to him, he tried to snatch it away. I got scared because I could see all his teeth, but I didn't say anything to Madame D'Eau about my father's dog guillotine.

It was dark inside Madame D'Eau's house, so dark I couldn't see very well at first, but there were all these cardboard boxes piled up everywhere. And inside the old pots and frying pans she put all the chewed up shoes she used to wear.

"*Assieds-toi*," she said. She made me sit down at her kitchen table. She could tell I was hungry. She set down two bowls and a hunk of bread. She poured me out hot soup.

"*Tu dois avoir faim.*" She gave me a big spoon, bigger than my mother's. "*Tiens, bouffes*," she said.

Her soup was so hot it burned my tongue, but she showed me how you have to spoon it from the edge of the bowl and keep turning the bowl around to get to the cool parts. She said if I wanted, I could even blow on it. It tasted so good, I wanted more. She threw up her hands and made a face because there wasn't any more. Then she did a funny little dance. "*Y'en a plus, y'en a plus*," she sang. She took the dishes and spoons and stuck them in the sink. Everywhere there were dirty dishes and dirty things piled up. In our house my mother was always complaining about what she called the filth. That's why she always wanted to have the painters, but she said you had to put things away, that way the painters didn't get paint over everything. I asked Madame D'Eau if she was putting things away because she was going to have the painters. She didn't understand.

"When the painters come. Are you putting all your things away for when the painters come?"

"*Ah, les peintres!*" When she laughed I could see all her side teeth were missing.

"*Non, ma cherie. Ce n'est pas les peintres!*" She told me how she had to move. She said how her old eyes couldn't see anymore which was why sometimes when Snow White did something nasty on the floor, she didn't pick it up until I told her it was there, and how her old teeth couldn't chew anymore, and that's why she had to eat soup all the time, and her old legs could hardly totter. She threw up her hands. "*Y'a la cervelle qui degringole*," she said, and she made me giggle because she said her brains were tumbling down.

"Are they going to fix you?"

"Fix me?"

"Where you're going?"

She let out a little shriek and she doubled over. I was glad I made her laugh, and then I could tell she wasn't laughing but I didn't say anything. She took a little white hanky out of her sweater pocket. When she was through blowing her nose, she reached her arms out for me to help her stand up. I never saw before how her hands were all twisted and knobbed like an old tree. I thought she was going to give me a hug, but she waved me away. *"Allez, allez,"* she said and she shooed me away the way she shooed Snow White. That's when she showed me how to plant the alligator pear. She took me to the window sill. "First you make a little hole, like this. Then you put the pit inside. Remember to put in just enough earth, not too much, and give it plenty of water at first so it will grow. Then you put it on the window sill where the sunshine always comes." She showed me one she had inside a glass that was already splitting open and you could see inside the crack a small green shoot was poking out. She promised I could have it when she went away.

We didn't get to have candles anymore after my mother went to work, but just in time, we got a Christmas tree with colored lights on it, all except purple because my mother said people don't usually like purple, but I liked purple best. They were big bulbs like the ones they had in the department stores. I liked to sit in the dark and watch them blink, and listen to my mother playing Christmas carols on her new piano. We sang songs about things like frankincense and myrrh. My father explained they were a kind of Christmas present the three kings gave the Baby Jesus, only people usually got them when they were supposed to die.

"Maybe they made a mistake," I said, but my father said they probably didn't because they were magicians and magicians have the gift of prophecy.

On Christmas Eve, I got to stay up late because my mother said it was vacation and she didn't have to make any etchings. After she put me to bed I was so turned upside down with all the songs and the lights going on and off, I couldn't even sleep. That's when I heard the doorbell ring. I could hear my mother answer. At first I thought maybe it was Mr. Pozo, but then I could tell it must be Madame D'Eau. I was trying to hear what she was saying but I couldn't because my door was closed. Then I heard it opening softly. *"Elle dort,"* my mother said, but I wasn't sleeping yet. If I just kept my eyes open a little bit, I could see Madame D'Eau. She was holding a big white envelope in her hand, the kind people send at Christmas time. In her other hand she had the pot with the alligator pear she promised me with a shiny ribbon on it.

I could feel my cheeks puffing up. I was happy in the dark, scrunched up under the covers, squinting my eyes. I wanted to see Madame D'Eau but I was trying not to let my eyelids move. I didn't want anyone else to know about our secrets, just me and Madame D'Eau. That's why I had to make believe I was already asleep.

Madame D'Eau tiptoed back out into the hallway. My mother closed my door. I wanted to jump out of bed and run after her, but then everyone would know I was only pretending, and I didn't want Madame D'Eau to know I lied. I heard my mother close the front door. That's how I could tell Madame D'Eau was gone.

The air was white when I woke up. It was very cold, even under the covers, but I ran to the window anyway. The glass was all bumpy like waves of rock candy with swirls and streaks sharp as knives on it, and there wasn't any way you could see out. I tugged at the window frame, I tried to lift. I pushed and pushed harder. The rotten wood and the flaking paint budged ever so little. A blast of cold air shot up the sleeves of my pajamas, but I didn't care because I could see outside and everything was white and still, and in between all the snowflakes whirling around, you could see a coat of white over everything, even my pink cake box with my chrysalis inside. Everything was gone: all the dirt and soot, all the gutters with their little scraps of paper and cigar butts and all the boxy cracker-jack cars, and the garbage cans lined up in rows. Everything was white, everything, all the lampposts with their milky glass lanterns, and the lacy iron fences and the banisters, all white and curly on the brownstone stoops. The world was playing make believe and everything got all hushed up.

Up the street, the milkman was rattling his empty bottles, lifting them back on his wagon. "Whoa!" he shouted to his horses so they would keep still long enough for him to get back on. I stretched my arm way out so the snowflakes could touch my hand. You could almost hear them landing with a kind of tiny plop. Plop. Plop, another one. And then another. Each one looked like a little tiny star, all lacy-sharp and splintery, some with points on them like swords, and some round like little fairy crowns, and small ones, all thin and spiky, got all mixed up together. They looked crunchy like slivers of glass, and shiny just like sugar icing, but when they touched my hand, they got all soft and left a tiny drop of water all melted on my hand.

I liked standing at the window. Even on rent day. I liked standing there with Madame D'eau waiting for the landlord. "Brahvemann." She always said his name in French, and she would nod her head. I don't know why she nodded like that, and I didn't ask her, but when she saw his chauffeur pulling up and opening the door, she would nod her head and take her little roll of money out of her old sweater pocket. She used to roll it up so tight, it looked like a green cigarette. She would flatten the money out and ask me to help her count it. She had to lick her finger because that way she said the money wouldn't stick. I said the numbers along with her. "*Un, deux, trois . . .*" and when we got to twenty-five, I used to shout, "*vingt-cinque*" very loud because Madame D'Eau said it was the very highest number anyone could ever count to when they were only four-maybe-going-on-five. That's what she said, anyway, and when she hugged me, her sweater smelled like dogs.

My mother told me Madame D'Eau had a daughter once, but she didn't know what happened to her. She said that's why Madame D'Eau had to go to a nursing home so people could take care of her. I asked my mother what it was like and if the people there would have to wear nursing shoes the way that stupid Helen in the beauty parlor did. But my mother said she didn't know.

I was getting really cold standing at the window, so cold I started shivering. I tried to push the window shut except it wouldn't budge. I tried pushing even harder. That's when my mother opened the door. She stood there staring at me with her eel-glass eyes. "What ahre you doing?" She said she always had to say her are's like that from when she learned to talk English from her aunt in London.

"What ahre you doing?"

"Watching the snowflakes falling down."

"Get away from there. At once! You're going to catch new monia!"

I didn't know what new monia was exactly, but I could tell it was something really bad because my mother said if you got it, you could even die. She made for the window to close it, but it got stuck. She pushed her dotted swiss curtains aside, the ones that smelled like soot. I watched her snap the window ropes. Smack. They slapped against the frame. Then she slammed the window shut.

"Get dressed. Right now, before you catch a cold. We're going downtown to get you a pair of shoes."

I didn't like to go downtown, but every time my shoes got chalky looking, especially the toes, that's when my mother said we had to go downtown but I told my mother they weren't very chalky looking yet.

"No smart talk. Get dressed at once and put on your shoes."

My mother pushed down hard on my toes. It made me say 'ouch,' except every time I said 'ouch,' like that we had to go downtown. I wished she could just let me watch the snowflakes falling. I wished we didn't have to go downtown. My mother didn't like to take the subway the way my father did. She said the subway was dirty, but the buses always made me sick and we had to always be in a hurry because my mother said there wasn't enough time to visit all the stores. We couldn't ever stop and look at all the ladies in black bonnets ringing bells or watch the dolls all dressed up in fur muffs ice skating in the windows. You could hear all the skater music but you couldn't ever really see because all the tall people were always standing up in front.

Every time we went downtown, my mother made me eat a warm breakfast with toast, and orange juice with a raw egg in it, and oatmeal with milk. Then I had to put on my snow suit. I could fasten all my buttons, but sometimes my mother still had to help me tie my laces. She helped me put my galoshes on because we were going out in a blizzard. She said it was even worse than the ones they had in Switzerland when they had to send out the St. Bernards to find all the people that got buried in the snow.

"How could the dogs find them if they got buried?"

"Because the dogs could smell them and then they gave them whiskey to warm up."

"Hurry," I told my mother. All the snowflakes were whirling around outside with all the patterns on them that I had to get to see. "Can't you hurry up?" I wished we didn't have to wait all the time it took her to get ready. But my mother didn't like to hurry. First she had to fight with her corset every time she tried to hook it up. Her brassiere hooks went clickclick like a ladder up her back but she always made me help her when she got up to the top one. She had to roll her silk stockings on very slowly so they wouldn't run and then she hitched them to her pink rubber garters. All the time the snowflakes kept falling and I couldn't get to see them because on went her thick woolen shirt and her matching woolen knickers. On went her satin slip that crackled and made blue sparks when she took it off at night. Then she stuck her head in her bright red woolen sweater, the one I wished she didn't wear because it made her front stick out. The blizzard was probably all over by now, but my mother still had to hold on to step into her skirt. Then she had to fix her hair and put her lipstick on. When she was done she took her fur coat out of the closet. My father said it was fur from baby lambs they had to take from inside their mothers before they even got born. It was all gray and crinkly, and my mother had to sew it up all the time because it kept getting cracks in it everywhere. She was almost ready. She just had to put on her favorite hat, the one she trimmed in black silk velvet. Her veil had tiny black pompons on it, and when she pulled it over her face, it looked like little flies were sitting on her nose. She turned from side to side looking at herself in front of the mirror. I could hear her sucking on her teeth. Now she was ready except she had to pull on her boots before she let me open the door.

That's when I remembered I didn't even thank Madame D'Eau for the alligator pear she gave me on Christmas Eve when I was pretending to be asleep, and the Christmas card with the lacy torn off edge and the red and purple anemones painted on the front. Her apartment door was open.

"Where are you going?"

"To see Snow White and Madame D'Eau."

"They aren't there," my mother said. "I told you they had to leave right after Christmas."

I could see down the hallway. Everything was gone, the runner where Snow White sometimes did his nasty things, and the leash that was always hanging on the parlor door, and all the boxes and the frying pans and pots with all the chewed up shoes in them, all gone, and through the doorway I could see clear down the hallway to the window sill, and the window box was gone with all the geraniums and alligator pears. Just the empty walls were left. They looked like cream of mushroom soup because Madame D'Eau never even got to have the painters.

The elevator came. The gate slid open. Inside was

someone tall I never saw before.

"Hi, sister!" He had this smile on him. It was even bigger than summer.

"How you doin', ma'am!" He smiled at my mother too.

My mother got very quiet. I could tell she didn't like the way he said things. My mother used to say people who talked like that were 'ordinary'.

"What's your name, sugar?"

I told him my name. I felt my mother tug my arm.

"You just call me Joe," he said. He turned around so he could see my mother. "You gonna take this chile right out into all that blizzard, mama?"

My mother shot him a chilly look. "We have to go downtown."

"I'm going to get new shoes."

"You gotta shoes, I gotta shoes. . . ." Joe started singing. We got to the floor where the lobby was. Joe swung open the gate to let us out.

"Couldn't we just watch the snow?"

"Hush." My mother shook my arm. "I don't want you making any fuss." Joe was dancing and singing the shoe song very loud but my mother pulled me along so fast, she wouldn't even let me watch.

My mother opened the lobby door. Outside it was still blizzarding. Up the street, the milkman was running, waving his arms and shouting "Whoa!" His horses ran right past us and on down the hill, pulling the milk wagon behind them. "Whoa!" The milkman kept shouting for them to stop. But the horses just went on clopclopping down the hill. The milkman was running fast, trying to catch up to them. "Whoa!" he kept shouting and he slipped and nearly fell.

Joe was standing right behind us, laughing. "He running like his pants on fire."

Just before the horses got to the big avenue, the milkman jumped on board. He grabbed the reins and gave a mighty tug. The horses shied. Steam was blowing out their nostrils.

"Them horses not goin' anywhere, no sir." Joe shook his head. The milkman was trying to make his horses giddyap. He was cursing and swearing something bad, but the snow was blowing in their eyes even with their blinders on, and they slipped and nearly fell. Joe turned to my mother. He gave her a big smile. "Mama? Mama, it blizzardin' out here somethin' fierce. The radio say there be no buses runnin'. It a devilish kind of mornin'."

My mother swept him a look. She wasn't going to listen to anybody, especially someone like him she didn't even know. She took hold of me. She gave Joe a stiff little smile.

"Mama," he said, "see if I'se right. All this mornin' I been hearin' on the radio. They be no buses nor no subways runnin'. Come on back inside and listen for yoself." He tried taking her arm. She shook him off. I couldn't tell at first what she was going to do. But then she let go of me. She went up the stoop stairs, back inside the lobby where it was warm. Joe held the door open for her. As she went past him, he winked at me.

"Watch out there, sister. Don't let none of them snowflakes get away!"

Just before supper, my father spread an old piece of red velvet on the kitchen table. This time he was getting ready to show off his dog guillotine but I wasn't scared anymore because Snow White was in the nursing home safe with Madame D'Eau.. He took my mother's cleaver away from her and stuck it in the slot. When he let go the rope, it fell with a thud and made the kitchen table shake.

"Emilio! Take that dreadful thing away at once and give me back my cleaver," my mother warned him. She was really mad, but my father wasn't listening. He kept lifting up the cleaver and letting go the rope. Wham, bang, slam, smash. My mother had enough. "Emilio!" she screamed, "*c'est assez. Assez. ASSEZ!*" She pushed my father away. She grabbed the head of cabbage she was going to make for supper. She tried to slice it with my father's guillotine. THWACK THWACKTHWACKTHWACK. "Look how well it cuts! Even better than the hobel we used to have in Switzerland!"

My father tried grabbing her by the arms, but my mother just went on cutting.

"It's even more efficient than the one we had at home!"

My father ran inside his room and slammed the door. We could hear him in there, shouting and cursing James Watt and the steam engine and progress and everything it stood for. When my mother ran and threw open the door, there was my father standing on his bed, smashing the frame on the floor with the picture of James Watt in it. Pieces of glass flew everywhere. My father picked the picture of James Watt up off the floor. He was tearing it into little tiny pieces and tossing them up in the air. "Cannibals!" he shouted, "cannibals! Cannibals, all of you!" He said progress was worthless, a delusion of mankind, one of its most insidious.

Because with people like my mother, progress was IMPOS-SIBLE. My mother said she didn't give a fig about progress. She said she was disgusted because he broke her picture frame. She told him if he could destroy her frame like he did, she was going to smash his guillotine to bits. My father said it was an accident. He promised to replace the glass, but he stuck a whole new photograph inside the frame. He said it was a picture of Charles Babbage and that Charles Babbage was a man to be trusted because he invented the Difference Machine that could add and subtract and multiply, and he had a Theory of Miracles which he even proved once by inventing shoes for walking on the water, just like Jesus did.

The buses were back running even though all the snow wasn't melted yet. When my mother found out, she made me eat a big breakfast even before I got dressed, but already when we were waiting for the elevator, I could feel the raw egg and the oatmeal trying to come up. When the elevator came, Joe slid open the gate.

"Hi, sugar!" Joe smiled at me. Something wiggled under his arm. It was a tiny puppy, all white everywhere with a black spot over one eye.

"What's his name?"

"Walter. He my Christmas present. Did Santa be nice to you too, sugar?"

He let me touch Walter. His ears were soft as peach fuzz, and inside they were all pink. Joe said he had to give him the bottle because he still missed his mama.

"Oh, could I please give him the bottle?"

My mother pulled her mouth in tight. She yanked my arm so I wouldn't say anything, but I wished Joe would let me give Walter his bottle and maybe even let me play with him a little bit. I wished the blizzard didn't stop so we couldn't go downtown.

Outside in the street, big mountains of snow were piled high everywhere. We had to go a whole six blocks to where the bus ran along the river. My mother had legs that were very long; that's how come she could go fast all the time. We had to climb over the snow drifts and jump past the puddles, with my mother pulling and tugging me along. I was nearly out of breath.

"Stop huffing and puffing. Keep your mouth closed," my mother said. We went even faster. I practiced making big clouds of steam come out of my mouth.

"I said keep your mouth closed. Don't let the cold air in." My mother wrapped my scarf tight around my face so I couldn't hardly see. I slipped and fell in a puddle of ice water where the snow already melted.

"Why can't you watch your step?" My mother was really mad now because I got everything soaked, my mittens and my leggings, and even my coat was sopping and water was even sloshing around inside my galoshes. She took her leather gloves off so she could slap the water off my coat. The bus raced by. It lifted wings of brownish slush and sprayed us both with water. She gave me a look out of her eel-glass eyes. "Now look what you made us do, we just missed the bus."

We had to wait and wait. Everything got cold, my arms and legs, and ribs and even my jaw began to shake. Another bus came. You could hear the motor wheezing and the engine coughed. It stopped where we were standing. The door squealed open. My mother grabbed me by the arm and pulled me up inside. The door slapped shut and the bus began to move.

"Hold on," my mother shouted. I watched the conductor make change from his little silver coin machine. Clickclickclick went his thumb. A little bunch of coins came out.

"We're going upstairs so you can see." My mother always liked to go upstairs. The steps were steep and she had to yank me up by the arm. I didn't like sitting on top of the bus. I could smell the gasoline up there and every time the bus stopped or started, it felt like I was going to be sick. My mother didn't like when I got sick because it messed up the floor and she said it embarrassed her to have to apologize to the conductor.

All up the stairs we left big crusts of melting snow that sank off our galoshes. The bus jerked ahead. We fell into our seats. At every stop the door sighed open and slapped shut again. The bus swayed and shook, and the motor growled and panted. People got on or sometimes they got off. You could see them out the window flopping in the snow.

When we got downtown, people were scraping snow into big heaps in the gutters. Just when we got off the bus, it started to snow again, but the snowflakes melted the second they fell on the ground. When they landed on my coat, they turned into tiny blobs of slush.

My mother said the day after Christmas was the best time for bargains. I couldn't tell what bargains were exactly but I guessed they must be brown with tongues in them and laces. The store lady made me take off my shoes and my galoshes. She made me stand on the metal shoe with the ears on it. My socks were wet but when she slid the front part under me, it tickled just the same. The lady said I could get off so she could read what size I was. But when we got the shoes, they were the kind you have to thread the laces in the holes crisscrosscrisscross without making a mistake or you have to start all over. They were brown and they went all the way up over my ankles exactly like my old ones did. My mother pulled my galoshes over them.

When we got out into the street, I asked her how come we left the old shoes with the lady, but my mother didn't answer, she just sucked on her teeth. That's how I could tell she had something on her mind.

"Aren't we going to go home?" But my mother wouldn't answer. We started walking along where we never went before. There were crowds of people carrying packages.

"What are they carrying all their presents for if it's already after Christmas?"

"They're taking them back."

"Back to where?"

"Back to the store."

I didn't have any presents except from Madame D'Eau and that was just before she had to go in the nursing home. I wished I didn't have to hide under the covers when she came. I wished I said something nice to her and thanked her, only I didn't tell her anything.

"Could we go see Madame D'Eau?"

My mother looked at me funny. "Madame D'Eau went to the nursing home."

"Yes, but can we visit her?"

"You don't want to go there."

"Yes, I do. I want to see Snow White."

"What an idea! They don't let dogs inside a nursing home. Snow White isn't even there."

"Where is he?"

"They put him to sleep."

I wanted to know where Snow White was sleeping, but when my mother said it, it made my stomach sink.

We got to this place where there was a park on one side and you could see all the people ice skating and spinning on the ice, but my mother didn't want to stop. We went past big gray houses with Christmas trees all lit up in the windows.

"Why don't the lights blink on and off the way ours do?"

"Because the people here are refined and they don't like their lights to blink," my mother said.

We came to a gray house. The front door was glass and it had all black iron bars with curly black designs. You could see inside to another door that had lace curtains on it. My mother rang the bell. We were standing in the doorway. It was warm there and you couldn't feel the wind.

"What are we waiting for?"

"For Gibby."

The door opened and there was someone tall and skinny with a fluffy pink angora sweater on and little pearls stuck in her ears.

"Mademoiselle!" She threw her arms around my mother. "Maddy's here," she called to somebody upstairs. "Oh, Maddy, dear, we've been expecting you!"

I never heard of Gibby before and she called my mother Maddy like she was someone else. I got this funny feeling in my stomach all of a sudden like we were in the elevator only I got off with the wrong double. It was the same floor. Everything looked the same, only you could tell it was all different.

We went inside. We had to go up some stairs, but if you wanted, you could ride up in a tiny elevator you had to sit down in. The parlor was all lit up with lamps with white shades on the tables everywhere and on the walls there were pictures of trees all feathery with summer leaves, and people in red riding coats riding brown horses with white stars on their foreheads, and little dogs running in between the horses' legs; you could tell they were yapping because their mouths were open, and they had on little white bibs, only they didn't look anything like Snow White or even Joe's little puppy, Walter.

You could see outside in the street through two big windows in the living room and inside was the hugest Christmas tree I ever saw. It was full of shiny glass balls and tinsel and stuff that looked like spider webs and caterpillar tents strung all over it, and underneath there were presents all wrapped up in colored paper and gold and silver ribbon. On the top was a kind of angel with a pink dress on and wings.

Gibby picked up one of the boxes and gave it to me. "One for you, and one for Maddy," she said.

I don't know what my mother got, but I got a tiny basket with lids that flapped open backwards like a book. It was all lined with blue silk quilting and little roses in the pattern, and tiny jars of jelly inside with lids with all different kinds of flowers on them. It even said something underneath. I showed it to Gibby. She had to hold it up high so she could look at it upside down. "It says 'Made in Indochina.'"

I didn't know what Indochina was for them to make such tiny baskets with duck feet made of tiny little matches that it stood on when you didn't want to carry it and you had to put it down.

Then Gibby was giving my mother all the presents she said they didn't want, and there was this big playpen with five dolls in it dressed all alike in different color pastel dresses. My mother said they were the quintuplets, and one of them even had my name embroidered on her dress. Gibby gave us green and red sour ball candy to take home, but we had to carry everything. Gibby said she would call a taxi, but my mother said no.

"Because it costs a lot."

My mother gave me a look. That's how I could tell I said something wrong. But Gibby just laughed. She hugged and kissed my mother one last time. Then we went out into the street. We had to carry all the presents on the bus. Our bags were so big, but we couldn't put them anywhere; we had to hold them on our laps so the people could sit down.

When we got home Joe took us upstairs.

"Where's Walter?" I asked him.

"Walter in his room."

That's how come I found out Walter had a room. When we got upstairs, my mother said how I was very tired, but first she said we had to pack all the dolls up so we could put them away till I got old enough to play with them. I asked her how old I would have to be, but my mother didn't say. She wrapped each one of them in tissue paper so their dresses wouldn't get mussed. One had on a mint green dress, but the one with my name had pink. I wished it was purple but my mother said pink was my best color on account of my skin, except I didn't like pink half as much as purple. Then she wrapped the playpen in brown paper after she stuck all the dolls inside.

My mother said she had to go to the butcher to buy something for dinner. I used to like going with her because the butcher had pickles floating around in a barrel, and sawdust on the floor you could make rivers and valleys in with your shoes, but best of all he liked to tell me the names of all the things he pulled out of their insides when he cut the chickens up. Once he even found a yellow egg yolk that the hen forgot to lay. I asked my mother could I go with her, but she said I was too tired and I had to take a nap. She told me not to get up and if anyone came to the door, not to answer the bell.

I couldn't go to sleep. I kept wishing I had a puppy just like Walter that I could give the bottle to. I wanted to see Walter's room. I didn't know where it was, but I wanted to find it so I could play with him. I got up and put my leggings on. I could even zip the legs down all the way like you were supposed to, and fasten all the buttons on my coat. I got into my new shoes, but I couldn't tie them very well, so I stuck my feet in my galoshes and kicked the shoes under the bed. I was going to go downstairs maybe for a bit, so I left the front door open just enough to get back in before my mother came. I pushed the elevator bell, but when the elevator stopped, it wasn't Joe. It was our super, Mr. Kepke.

"Where's Joe?"

"Down in the basement."

Mr. Kepke didn't talk much. He smelled like cigars and he breathed very loud like he was snoring. I listened to him breathing all the way down to the basement.

"Just go down there." He pointed down the white-washed corridor. There was this room off to one side with all newspaper on the floor. Inside Joe was sitting on the bed. You could even see the bedsprings under his woolen blanket. He was giving Walter his bottle.

"Hi, there, sugar!"

"How come you put newspapers all over the floor?"

Joe laughed. "That's so Walter learn where to do his business."

Walter was drinking from a real baby bottle; it even had a rubber nipple on it. He was lying all curled up with his fat little body wrapped around himself. He kept smacking his tail against the blanket. When I touched his fur it felt all soft.

"How come you call him Walter?"

"Because he Walter." Joe said I could give Walter the rest of his bottle. I could feel him sucking on it hard till all the milk was gone and when Joe took away the bottle, he chewed on my finger with his tiny baby teeth. When he stood up, he even licked my face.

"You better get along home now, sugar, 'cause I gotta go back to work."

"Could you let me mind Walter while you run the elevator up and down?"

"Walter all right in his room," Joe said and he took me back upstairs.

I didn't know what to do because where we lived, the door was locked and I couldn't get it open. I went back and pushed the elevator button. Joe came back up.

"What's the matter, sugar?"

"I can't get back inside."

Joe looked like he could tell what you were supposed to do, but when we got to my door and he rang the bell, nobody came.

"Your mama gone out. You come on down, sister. We'll go get Mr. Kepke."

Mr. Kepke grumbled a lot, but he gave Joe a special key that's supposed to open any door so Joe could let me back inside.

"If my mother says Walter can come visiting, then could I maybe play with him?"

This big laugh burst out of him. "So long's he ain't waterproof, Walter still have to play outside."

But my mother kept saying there was too much snow

to let me play outside. She made me play inside in the living room with my stuffed animals instead. My mother had this big trunk with stickers on it from all the places she went to visit. There was even one with a picture of London Bridge from when she went to learn English from her aunt. Inside it had pieces of silk and royal blue shiny stuff that she said I could use to play with and all her upholstery samples from when she was an interior decorator, and a box of old jewelry with a brooch Madame D'Eau gave me with green and blue and pink colored pearls on it and diamonds. I got my panda all dressed up and I had a monkey named O-Mee-Oh who had safety pins on his feet because he liked to ice skate. I dressed them up for the monkey's wedding. I even had a stupid polar bear named Prudence with a silly apron on. I let her be the priest, except my mother said to call her a minister. But I still didn't know what people were supposed to say when they were getting married. My mother was busy cooking supper in the kitchen so I had to ask my father, but he was busy making something in his room. It was something white and lumpy like oatmeal sometimes gets, but he was putting newspaper in it because he said you had to leave it soaking overnight. He had on big red rubber gloves that made him look like he had lobster claws. He was sticking all these pieces of gloppy stuff with newspaper on a giant red balloon.

"You can come in but don't make a racket," he said, "or you'll spoil my concentration."

"How come you're ruining the balloon like that?"

He said he needed to because he was making the world, and it had to be round.

"What for?"

"Why does it have to be round?"

"No. What do you need a world for?"

"Because you have to have a world before you can put things in it."

I made him come out in the living room so he could see Panda with her turquoise veil on waiting to be married.

"Aha!" he said, "that reminds me of a story: Once upon a time there was a Panda who came from a big place named China and a monkey named O-Mee-Oh, who came from a place called Africa where it was very hot. That's why he had to wear ice skates in New York, because of the snow and ice. Where he came from in Africa there were lots of friendly monkeys, but he was cold and lonely in New York because there weren't any monkeys like him to play with, just animals who were black and white and shivering all the time. He needed somebody to iron his shirts and keep him warm and make the bed. That's why he had to marry Panda right away."

That was the story my father said. I asked him what people were supposed to say when they had to get married. My father said it was enough just to say: "do you, Panda, take this ape as your lawful wedded wife" And then Panda had to say "I do." But my father made a mistake because how could O-Mee-Oh be the bride if O-Mee-Oh was a boy? When I told him he made a mistake, my father just laughed and laughed. So I got the pearl brooch out so I could pin the veil on O-Mee-Oh because my father said he had to be the bride. Prudence was ready in her stupid apron.

"Do you, Panda, take this ape for your awful wedded wife?"

"Lawful," my father corrected. He even answered for Panda. "I do," he said.

Then it was Panda's turn to be the bride, but my father said we had to stop the wedding because it was getting all mixed up. He threw all my animals in my mother's trunk with London Bridge on it, and slammed the lid down tight. He even made believe he was turning the key, except there wasn't any lock.

"What are you doing that for?"

"So they can't come back and bother me!"

After that he wouldn't let me come back inside his room. I wished I could see what he was making. Every time he had to go to work, I would pretend I was knocking on the door. "Can I come in now?" Sometimes he wouldn't answer, but other times he opened the door. I used to pretend he let me go inside and watch.

"Shhhh," he always said, "don't talk so loud. You'll spoil my concentration." But he just said it so my mother wouldn't hear. He always put my chair up close so I could sit and watch. It was too high off the floor for me and my feet had to swing back and forth, back and forth, and sometimes they kicked against the rungs. But even though I didn't do it on purpose, he would tell me to be quiet.

"What are you making?" I would ask him. But it wasn't always a good thing to ask because sometimes the room would disappear with my father in it.

But my father had to stop making things because one time when he went to work my mother threw all his newspapers out. When he came home I was supposed to be asleep, but I could hear him in the hallway telling her how he had saved up papers for years and years and years, and how he was going to cut them out when he had time, and after he finished, he was going to turn all the left-over newspaper into papier maché, and use all the left-over words to make crossword puzzles. He told her what she did was worse than stealing the crutches from a drowning man. So my mother said how she couldn't stand his dirt, his filth and all his mess. She said because of him the cockroaches were getting so pushy every night they were lining up at the dinner table begging for scraps. And she had to go to work, she didn't have time to always keep bashing at them with her broom. He was whispering, but I could hear every word he said because he was grinding every one of them between his teeth. He was telling her the things he was going to do to her because she threw his newspapers out when he wasn't looking, and now the cockroaches had nowhere left to go. Then she said something about Mr. Pozo, and I could hear my father stomp down the corridor to his room and slam the door. After that I could hardly go to sleep. Then I had this dream. I was sitting on my chair in my father's room. He had a box on his table that looked black and shiny, and around it little pointy lights like the ones my mother had for the Christmas tree, except they were ocean-colored, and inside there was this kind of moony light. He dragged my chair even closer so I could stand on it and watch. Somebody was inside the box, but I couldn't tell who it was, but then it started to look like it was me, except it was just a shadow of me looking down inside it. There wasn't any water on it, but it felt cold like the fluoroscope that time my mother took me to be x-rayed so I wouldn't get tuberculosis, except it didn't hum or buzz. When I looked inside, my father was in there where I was supposed to be, only it looked like me, but it looked like my father, too. It didn't exactly look like me any more, but it wasn't my father either.

"What's it supposed to be?"

"Shhhh! Don't talk so loud! It's my Difference Machine."

At breakfast I couldn't even eat my cereal. "You woke me up last night. I could hear you talking. I could hear everything you said." It just popped out of my mouth like that. My father didn't say anything, he didn't even look at me. My mother was pretending she didn't even hear.

"How come Mr. Pozo never comes to visit any more?"

Nobody said anything except all of a sudden my mother threw the spoon smack into my bowl. Oatmeal splashed over everything.

"Go to your room," my mother shouted. "Go to your room at once!"

"But I didn't do anything."

"Go to your ROOM!"

"But Purtzi," my father said, "she hasn't done anything naughty."

My mother got even madder. She yanked open the ironing board. She plugged the iron in. She swept one of my father's shirts out of the laundry basket. She slammed the iron down on the collar. It started hissing and sputtering. The collar turned brown and there was this burning smell. My mother started screaming. She screamed and screamed and screamed. My father unplugged the iron. He kept making noises like a chicken. "P-p-please, P-p-purtzi, p-p-please think about the neighbors."

"To hell with the neighbors. *Je les emmerde*, the neighbors. They can choke on their own piss!" My mother threw the kitchen window open wide. She leaned as far as she could without falling out into the courtyard. She was screaming and screaming and screaming and screaming. "You can all go to hellhellhell!" Every scream bounced off the courtyard walls, and every brick shouted back a hundred little hells. It made a tearing noise like the butcher sawing bones. I wished I didn't have to hear it.

My father pulled her back inside and slammed the window shut. Then he tried clucking at her to make her stop.

My mother turned to my father. "I want her to get down on her knees this very minute and not get up until she says she's sorry. Get down this very minute and apologize!"

My father flapped his hands the way he did when he was trying to get her to be quiet. "Purtzi," he said, "be reasonable."

"Be reasonable, be reasonable! What did you ever do to make me be reasonable? If I was reasonable, where would we be?" She started crying. I couldn't tell if she was crying over all the laundry that needed to be ironed, or over her knuckles that were bleeding from all the washing she had to do. But maybe it was because she could tell I could hear every word my father said to her long after he was through saying them. I could even hear them echo when I was supposed to be asleep.

My father shooed me out of the kitchen and he closed the door so it didn't make any sound. Outside in the hall he said if I wanted us to take my animals out of the trunk so we could play with them again.

I looked at my father. He looked like God, only he was sadder.

"Why did you have to marry my mother?" He didn't answer when I asked him. So I said, "What did you marry her for?" I could tell he heard me, but he didn't say anything. He just went back inside his room and shut the door.

My mother still had vacation. She didn't have her etchings, and she didn't have to go back to work. She said she was going to the nursing home to visit Madame D'Eau. I told her I wanted to come too.

"They don't allow any children, only old people," my mother said. My mother wasn't very old and she was going but she just sucked on her teeth when I said it. She told me I had to stay at home. I didn't want to play with my stuffed animals anymore, but I didn't say anything because I really wanted to play with Walter, and maybe look in my father's room to see if I could find Mr. Pozo's book. I waited till after she was gone. I got my leggings on. I fastened all the buttons on my coat. I put on my hat with the stupid ear muffs on it, and I stuck my shoes inside my galoshes so no one could tell I didn't really tie them.

Even before the elevator came, I could tell it was Joe because I could hear him whistling. He slid open the gate.

"Where you goin', sugar?"

I got inside. "My mother says I can play outside."

We started going down. He looked at me kind of funny. "I jus' took your mama down."

"Unhunh. That's why she wants me to play outside till she gets back. So now can I play with Walter?"

"I got no leash for him jus' yet. He only a puppy."

"Oh, not in the street! My mother says I have to play downstairs in the courtyard."

"Well, O.K., sugar. But only till it's time for him to have his milk."

Joe took me down to the basement so we could get Walter out of his room. He was wagging his new moon tail when he saw us, and he did this little bow and stretched his hind legs out one at a time. Joe even put a sock on him to keep him warm outside. He trotted with us through the basement corridor and out into the courtyard.

"You make him stay right here, sugar. Jus' throw him his ball, but don't be letting him get in no corridors or nothin' so's there won't be any trouble."

The snow was still frozen in sooty patches in the courtyard because the sun never got all the way down there.

I threw Walter his ball, but every time he caught it, he wouldn't give it back. I had to wiggle it out of his mouth every single time. I could tell he liked chewing it better than he liked me throwing it. So I just squatted in the snow and petted him. I told him a story about a stubborn puppy who wouldn't let go his ball.

Way up on the fourth floor where we lived, you could see where the sun was shining, but down in the shade where I was playing with Walter, it stayed cold and you could hear the wind whooing through the basement, chasing down the corridors till it blew into the courtyard.

It got so cold, I wished I could go back inside, but I couldn't remember which way you were supposed to go to get to the elevator because we came a different way. Joe said only play with Walter in the courtyard, but I started pushing the doors open anyway, looking in the corridors to see if I could tell which way to go. I had to keep Walter from running inside with my foot. You couldn't see anything in there because it got dark when you got too far inside. I was just pushing this one door open when a light came on way down the other end. And there was Mr. Kepke. He was cursing something really bad, but I couldn't tell what he was shouting because the echoes were bouncing everywhere and I couldn't see who he was yelling at, just Mr. Kepke at the end of the corridor where it turned the corner. Then there was this noise like glass breaking and something hit Mr. Kepke right in the face, but I couldn't tell what it was, and Mr. Kepke stuck his hand out and it was bleeding and bleeding. Walter was trying to get inside, but Joe said not to let him, and anyway I got really scared.

Still Joe didn't come for Walter and it got so cold, I wanted to stop playing and go home. Then the lunch time whistle blew, and Joe came running into the courtyard.

"Come on, sister. It time to go!" He grabbed Walter and tucked him under his arm. He took me by the hand. "We gotta get you home."

I couldn't tell why we had to be climbing all the stairs, but Joe said it was because the elevator quit running.

"Come on, sugar, jus' one more flight."

"Do you have the key?" but I could tell he didn't hear. "The key for getting me back inside."

"Un-unh," Joe shook his head. "There ain't no more key. This time you gotta wait till your mama come home. Where she at?"

I couldn't tell when my mother would come back because she was in the nursing home visiting Madame D'Eau. Joe looked at me. "She won't be long now, sugar."

He stood me on the doormat. "Wait right here. Your mama gonna come along any time now."

I could see Walter's little white body wriggling under Joe's arm. His tail was wagging, and Joe was running to the stairway door. He kicked it open.

"So long, sugar."

I ran after him. "I have to tell Walter good-bye." But I could tell he didn't hear me because the door swung shut. I could hear Joe tromping down the stairs, two at a time. Our front door opened. My father was standing there.

"Where have you been?"

"Downstairs."

"Where's your mother?"

"She had to go to the nursing home to visit Madame D'Eau . . ."

My father looked at me funny.

". . . so she let me play downstairs in the courtyard." I didn't say about Walter or Mr. Kepke in the basement or what I saw or anything.

"Get inside," my father said. He started helping me off with my galoshes, and putting my snowsuit on the radiator so it could dry out.

"How come Mr. Pozo never comes any more?"

"Because it's still vacation time."

"And Mr. Pozo has vacation?"

My father laughed. "No. Your mother has vacation because the etching school is closed."

"But then why doesn't Mr. Pozo come?"

My father sighed. "Mr. Pozo doesn't come because your mother can't speak Spanish."

"And if Mr. Pozo came, she couldn't talk any Spanish?"

My father nodded.

"What's the name of Mr. Pozo's book? Does it have a name in Spanish?"

My father said, yes, it was called *Locuras*.

"What does *'locuras'* mean?"

My father said it means crazy things.

"What kind of crazy things?"

"Oh, all sorts of things."

"But Mr. Pozo isn't crazy."

My father was laughing really hard. "No. Mr. Pozo is a devil, but Mr. Pozo isn't crazy."

"Does everything in the world have all different names in Spanish?"

My father said nearly everything.

"But is there some language where people don't have to have names in it for everything?"

My father wrinkled his forehead. He said every language has words in it for nearly everything, and some languages even have words in them for words.

"But could there be a language where people don't have to say words for things all the time?"

My father didn't answer. He made me stand by the window and hold my arm up high enough so the sun could shine on it.

"What do you see?"

I could see little tiny hairs all over my arm.

"Look carefully," my father said.

I looked closer. Between all the little cracks and tiny mountains on my skin it had all rainbow colors, pink and yellow and green and even blue.

My father nodded. He looked at me quietly for a long time. "Rainbows are the viaticum of angels," he whispered. "So says the Kabbala of Angels: their skin is clothed in light." But he said a person's skin was nothing compared to the skin of an angel because angels, as they were meant to be, as the Great Ones had intended, were celestial beings, clothed in blinding radiance and terrifying majesty, except when I asked him what their clothes looked like, my father wouldn't say. He just made me turn around and face the wall. When he said I could look again, he had Mr. Pozo's book. He opened it to a place that had a crinkly kind of tissue paper. When he peeled the paper back, it had the picture of an angel and all over it had eyes, all over its skin, only the blackest, blackest eyes, so black they didn't have any bottoms inside them because my father said that only in the perfect darkness of the divine could people ever hope to find any light. It had eyes all over its hands and feet and arms and legs, and in the center of its forehead, and even on the thing it had hanging between its legs.

"What's that?"

But my father snapped the book shut so quick, I nearly got my finger caught.

My mother got Hermine to be with me for when she had to go back to work so I wouldn't stay alone. My mother said Hermine was a governess, but I just called her Hermine. Her hair was blonde and long because she said her mother never made her cut it, and after we had breakfast, she let me brush it with the silver brush with the real pig bristles on it that came with her from Germany. I asked her how they could stick the pig bristles in so tight they stayed inside the brush.

"They take the pig by the tail and hold him very still."

Hermine even had a leather suitcase that said Bremerhaven on it. She said it was the place you had to go when you had to take the boat. At breakfast, she liked to spread big chunks of butter on her toast, but when my mother scolded her for taking such big pieces, Hermine just said butter was very good for you and cream was even better. She had to sleep with me in the big room so I had to lie very still at night and pretend to be asleep. But what I really liked was the way she took me to the park to feed the squirrels because they were starving in the snow and they didn't have anything to eat. One time we even saw a baby bird lying in the snow, all wrinkled up inside a broken shell. It had an ugly looking beak, and its feathers were all sticky from the egg. I told Hermine with wings like that all bare and sticky, how could the bird ever learn to fly. Hermine pulled me away.

"Don't be silly. Every bird looks like that at first. So did you. Come on."

Every time we had to cross the street, Hermine got

so scared I had to hold her hand. "Watch out, *passen sie auf*," I used to say to her. I liked to say things to her in German because every time she smiled, you could see her silver tooth. One time I even saved her from an old scraggly man who wanted to kiss her in the street. My father liked to kiss her, too.

I kept wishing I had blonde hair just as long and straight as Hermine's and she would let me use her silver brush to brush it, the one that came with her from Germany with the genuine pig bristles. I really liked Hermine and my father liked her, too. I never heard him laugh so hard as when Hermine got to eat with us. One time at supper, he told her how there were invisible lines all over the world where things underwent a mysterious change. He told her how when you caught brightly colored fish like they had in National Geographic, within minutes they lost all their color because they only had color deep underneath the water, but once they got fished out, even though people could see them better, they didn't have any color any more.

Hermine just smiled at him and showed her silver tooth.

I really liked Hermine. Once I even told her about the time when it gets dark, and everything looks like cut-outs because nothing has color any more and the sky turns this kind of dizzy light, so green it makes you feel like you want to fall up in it, only it isn't really green, but it isn't blue either, and this icy winter star comes out, and I said how nobody in the world, not even one single person could tell what color it was, but I would tell her the name if she promised not to tell. I brushed her long blonde hair away so I could whisper in her ear. She couldn't hear what I was saying, so I whispered it again, but a little louder. She still couldn't tell what it was supposed to be.

"Fishlight," I said.

"*Ach! Fischleucht!*" She laughed and clapped her hands and her eyes popped open so wide they looked like little balls.

During the long afternoons when my mother was at work, Hermine would go in the parlor and sit at my mother's new piano. She would practice something she called *Lieder, jah?* She would open her mouth really big, and then she would start to sing. My father even started coming out of his room to listen to her play. She had that way of squeezing the music out. It sounded like if a cow could purr. I felt sorry for her when she had to sing like that because it must really hurt, and the piano sounded so sad and far away, sometimes it even made me cry and Hermine would squeeze and squeeze. That's when my father would open the French doors, or sometimes he would just peek through the silk curtains that my mother hung over the door so she could have 'privacy' because when Hermine came, the living room got turned into my mother's bedroom.

Sometimes my father would even tiptoe in and sit down. Hermine pretended she didn't even hear him, but she squeezed even harder. And when Hermine's song would be over and she would play the last chord, my father clapped and clapped, and Hermine would turn around and act all surprised to see my father sitting there, and her face would break out into smiles and you could see her silver tooth.

Sometimes my father made her go back and play the last chord. He held up a warning finger so she could hear the invisible lines in the world where he said everything changed. You could hear the music get farther and farther away before it disappeared, but it was never as good as when Hermine played the whole song all over again.

When it got very dark, my father wouldn't turn on the lamp. He kept talking to Hermine in the dark. One time he said he was going to make Hermine something really special that when you spin it, it would go from black and white to all the colors of the rainbow.

I asked him, "Like what?"

"You'll see," my father said.

But no one ever did because the next day Hermine had her leather suitcase open on the bed. She was putting everything inside, even the silver brush that came with her from Germany with the genuine pig bristles. She was crying and crying.

I tried to cheer her up. "*Passen sie auf,*" I said to her but she just gave me a nasty look. I got her some tissues and she cried even harder so I went to the kitchen to get her a piece of bread. The butter was too hard for me to even cut it, so I just put the whole piece on top of it. Then I took it to Hermine but she pushed it away so hard, the butter fell down on the carpet and got dust all over it but I picked it up anyway and put it back so my mother wouldn't find out I took it.

"What's the matter?"

"I have to go away." She pressed the bunch of hankies I got her to her nose. She was sobbing and sobbing.

I started to cry too. I really liked Hermine.

When my mother came home, I asked her how come we couldn't have Hermine anymore. My mother said my father got a job and now she didn't have to go to work, she could stay at home with me.

I missed Hermine. I wished she didn't have to go. I wished my father didn't have to go to work so he could stay at home and play with me, and maybe take me out. I didn't want to stay home just with my mother because she made me take naps all the time and she never let me do things. She said it was too cold to play out in the courtyard where the stray cats came sometimes, and I couldn't go visiting because Snow White and Madame D'Eau were gone.

The only time my mother ever went out was after vacation was over when she went back at night to the school to make her etchings. She let me watch her put her purple lipstick on and before she put her coat on with the fur from all the baby lambs that weren't even born, she let me help her on with her galoshes because outside it was snowing. I was in my pajamas already, but I kept waiting because if Mr. Pozo came after my mother went out, then maybe my father would let me stay up late. A little while after she went out, the door bell rang. My father ran to answer it. He let me say good night to Mr. Pozo in the living room — say " '*buenas noches*' to Mr. Pozo," my father said — but after that I had to get in bed so my father could tuck me in.

I could see Mr. Pozo standing behind my father in the corridor. He blew me a kiss. Then my father put out the light and shut the door. For a long time I could hear them talking in the living room, and then it got all quiet.

When I woke up it was dark, but I could hear my mother screaming. I couldn't tell where it was coming from, but her voice kept getting louder. I didn't know why she was screaming in the night like that because she always used to scream in the daytime when people were awake. I got really scared because she came into my room and my father came in after her.

"P-p-purtzi, p-p-please. . . ." He was trying to make

her be still, but my mother just went on screaming in the dark.

"P-p-purtzi, p-p-please, think of the child. . . ."

"I am thinking of the child. Get out, you rat, you miserable bastard. Get out. Get out right now. And tell that filthy scum to get out, too, and take his dirty pictures with him." She kept screaming and screaming and hitting him in the chest. She was pushing him out of my room back into the hallway. She kept hitting him all the way down the corridor.

"P-p-please, P-p-purtzi," he kept saying, "please be reasonable." He was trying to make her listen. I was really scared. I never heard her scream in the night like that before. My mother caught me watching. "And you! Mind your business. Get back to bed!" she screamed at me, "and close your door." But she didn't come after me. She just kept pushing my father down the hall. "Get out," she screamed, "get out, and neverevereverever come back!"

The front door went bang. I couldn't tell what happened but my mother was still crying. I was crying, too. She came back inside my room. She sat down on my bed.

"Why can't my father ever come back?"

"Stop crying and get back to sleep," my mother said.

"But I want my father to come back."

"He can't ever come back." That's what my mother said. She said he couldn't come back because she didn't want him to. Then she went away.

I kept crying and crying. My pillow got all wet, and all the tissues got all soggy because I kept blowing into them. I couldn't stop. I was hiccoughing and hiccoughing, and I had a stomach ache because all that crying made me sick, and I kept thinking why did my father have to go away. I wished my mother didn't have to be my mother anymore, if only she could just be somebody else's mother. I wished he

could still be my father the way he was when he told me
stories and he played with me and took me with him to the
park or down 125th Street to see all the people in their
fancy hats and Chesterfields and all the trumpet players who
said 'hi', because the sun was out and the morning was all
shining, and I was walking with my father, and he held me
by the hand. Pleasegodohplease, makemyfathercomeback,
please, I kept saying over and over again because I couldn't
stop.

After my father went away, first I caught a cold. My mother
made me stay home from school. She kept packing things
up and putting everything in boxes. I couldn't tell why she
was doing it, but then she said she didn't want the painters
to mess up all her things, and she was going to hide everything in the closet where the painters couldn't see it. She
had silver dancing shoes with precious stones on them she
used to wear a long time ago when my father used to take
her dancing, and an amber necklace with beads on it as big
as eggs. She even had a fan with real tortoise shell ribs, and
an evening bag with diamonds she never let me play with.
She was putting everything away. She put blankets and tape
all over her new piano so it looked like it had an accident.
Then she took all the pictures down, even the picture my
father had of Charles Babbage inventing the Difference Machine. She took everything down, even the curtains. She
shoved my father's easy chair into the middle of the room
with all the other furniture. She lifted the seat cushion to
pound out the dust. Underneath was a book covered with
black leather. My mother picked it up. A bunch of pictures

fell out with all naked people in them. It looked like they were taking a bath, only there wasn't any water.

"Don't look." My mother said for me to leave the room. She started ripping the pictures up in little tiny pieces and tearing up Mr. Pozo's book.

"Stop!"

"Get out," she screamed. "I told you not to look."

"But that's Mr. Pozo's book!"

She grabbed me by my ear and shook me. "What do you know? Don't you ever, don't you evereverever tell me what to do. Don't you ever try it." She shook me over and over. I was crying and coughing and my ear really hurt.

She jerked me loose. She was already in the kitchen opening up the dumbwaiter. She threw everything down there. I could hear this big thud when it landed in the basement.

"That was Mr. Pozo's book," I said.

"Mind your business now," she said. "And stop crying."

She made me help her pile everything on the bed. First she put the mirror upside down with all the faded roses on it, and over it she piled the playpen with all the dolls in matching dresses on that I wasn't old enough to play with, and all the rollers and things she used to fix her legs with when no one was watching, and all her boxes of lace and the bags with all her appliqué roses, and the Christmas carols and the Schubert piano pieces that she used to like to play, and all the hatboxes with her hats in them and my father's Homburg that she used to say made him look so distinguished when he wore it in the street.

The turquoise silk curtains were still hanging on the French doors from when Hermine came to stay with us so my mother could have 'privacy'. She had to get up on the rickety stepladder so she could take them down. She made me stand real close to her because she didn't want to fall.

My cold kept getting worse. My mother made me get in bed. I had to lie with a hot water bottle all tucked inside the blankets listening to the ticking of the clock. It got so bad, we couldn't even have the painters. I didn't care about Walter any more or my color crayons or my alligator pear that Madame D'Eau gave me, or all the paper my father got for me to draw my orange and magenta roses on, and all my ladies with hoop skirts and tulips growing out of them. I even forgot about my cake box with the chrysalis inside, and O-Mee-Oh, and my stupid polar bear, and Panda. I forgot all of them.

My mother made me stay in bed. She put a steam machine inside my room. In the night, I could hear it whispering and all day long I could watch the steam jets coming out and disappearing in the air. When I fell asleep I had this dream. My father was sitting in his easy chair under his reading lamp. He was looking at Mr. Pozo's book. But every time he turned the page, little puffs of dust came out all bright and silvery, and started floating in the air, only they turned into tiny bugs with wings that you could see through, but their bodies were all pink and their legs were rubbery like Mr. Pozo's doll. They kept swirling higher and higher until my father's room began to spin. But every time they knocked against the light bulb, their wings got burnt and you could hear them sizzle. They scattered over everything, over the doilies on my father's chair and the stacks of newspapers and books my father had piled up all over the floor, and even on my father's head. Their legs were still wriggling and their wings rattled like paper when it crumples up. My mother kept sweeping them up in little piles, and when she threw them down the dumbwaiter, she had to slam the door quick because fiery sparks flew up.

I was sitting in my father's lap. I put my arms around his neck. "Why can't you just stay home?"

He pointed to a word in Mr. Pozo's book, but I didn't know what it said.

"Why can't you?"

But my father said he couldn't.

I kept coughing and coughing. My mother called the doctor. He made me stick my tongue out and he put his finger on my wrist so he could count my pulse. He was standing in the hallway talking to my mother. They were whispering something, but I could hear what they were saying. I got really scared because the doctor said I had new monia and my mother told me how people who got new monia died, and my bed kept rocking up and down, and the doctor couldn't stop it. Sometimes my feet went up so high, I whooshed out like a wave, but other times when my mother came in to bring me water to drink, my neck wasn't long enough to lift my head up any more.

Whoosh, I would float out into a wave of light, except it was dark, darker than night, but you could breathe and see in it like air. And somewhere the moon was shining, but it was coming from the room next door, except there was no door, and there wasn't any room, just the one with me inside hanging upside down and there was this drumming noise and it kept drumming the way it does when you lie in the dark sometimes and you can't tell where it's coming from.

My father was making something on his work table under his gooseneck lamp. He was making a little box out of the ribs of my mother's ballroom fan. I watched him rip the satin ribbon out. The spokes fell to the table with a clatter. I watched him with his long clipping shears, cutting and snipping, piling up little pieces of silk. And when they fell on the table, they didn't make any noise because he was cutting up my mother's satin underwear in little tiny squares so he could pad the bottom and the edges of the box.

"What are you doing that for?"

But he put his finger to his lips. "Shhhh. You'll scare all my little angels."

Everywhere people were getting ready, putting green sheets over everything so nobody could see, and the dumb-waiter bell kept buzzing because something was supposed to happen, but my father just went on fitting the corners snugly, padding the tiny box with cotton. He picked up something with my mother's tweezers. It looked like my chrysa-lis. He stuck it with my mother's pearly hatpin. Something brown oozed out of it. "Frankincense and myrrh," he said and he was smelling it and laughing his sawdust laugh the way they do it in the House of Wax. He took hold of my finger and made me touch it. A moon-colored dust spilled over my hand.

There wasn't any light left because I kept breathing it, only I wasn't breathing air, it was only water, and there were tiny lights in it everywhere like somebody stuck hat-pins in the night, but it wasn't like stars or snowflakes or anything because the light was coming from the other room, and outside I could see my mother's bright red hair. I could tell it was her. She kept trying to reach inside, but her arm wasn't long enough. and she was wringing out the washrag so she could sponge me off, but she couldn't reach, and she was wringing and wringing it, and I was alone out there, rocking my head back and forth, back and forth on the pil-low. I kept wishing I could get back inside only I couldn't remember the word you were supposed to say, and I couldn't sit up because the room was floating and the bed was tilting and I was falling in a wave of light.

My mother was sitting on a chair alone in the lamp-light. I could see the white enamel basin with the glue in it and all the bottles with the red and orange stuff in them, and the fat spoon lying on the white towel with the stripes on it. Outside somebody kept shouting something, jerking the washlines back and forth. I could hear the pulleys squealing in the dark. They were hanging shoes out there and galoshes, yanking and pulling and shouting something, only I couldn't tell what they were saying, I was scared the line would break and my shoes would fall down in the court-yard, and people kept shouting:

"Liiiiilye-e-e."

"Viiiiiiiolet."

"Rooooooooses."

Outside it smelled like rain, only the sun was shin-ing. The sky was raining feathers. They kept floating down in the courtyard. It made a noise like bees buzzing, and I could hear horses clipclopping in the street and cartwheels rolling along the cobblestones.

My mother opened the window wider. I could feel the soft air blowing her dotted swiss curtains, the ones that smelled like soot. Down in the street peddlars were calling out the names of flowers. My mother went down to buy me a hyacinth. It was pink, and when she came back, she put it on my windowsill so I could see it from my bed.

A hand was lying on the blanket. I couldn't tell if it was my hand, but then I remembered my fingers. They were mine. And my hand. And my arm. Everything looked new: the specks of dust floating in the air, the curtains bal-looning in the sunlight, the bright turquoise on my bed-room walls, the way the blanket had all these little balls on it everywhere, and the sheets smelled like burning. Everything felt the same, only it was different.

"Sit up," my mother said.

I tried sitting up but my elbows got lost and my neck felt all wilted. She put her arms around me to help me sit up. She kept holding me and giving me water to drink and this sound was coming out of her and I could hear her swallowing.

My father came to visit me. He was sitting on my bed. He kept saying how proud he was because I asked my mother for a baby bottle when I couldn't sit up to drink.

"But promise you won't ever tell anyone, not even Mr. Pozo."

My mother shot him one of her eel looks, but he didn't even see it.

She said I should try to get out of bed. When she pulled the covers back, my legs looked all small and spindly like they belonged to someone else. My mother helped me slide over the bed sheets, but when I tried to stand up, my feet forgot the floor and my father had to catch me.

I could see the pink cake box outside the window, sitting on the sill. I wanted to see if my chrysalis got hatched, but my mother said she had to take me to the toilet.

"Purtzi, Purtzi," my father said, "please let her see."

But when we got back from the bathroom my mother made me lie down. She tucked me back inside the covers and she shut the door very quietly the way she used to do when she thought I was asleep. I waited till I couldn't hear her any more. Then I lifted the covers and slid my feet onto the floor. I had to hold onto the edge of the bed till I got close enough to reach outside the window for the box. I opened the lid.

Inside was all gray, gray cardboard, gray twig, the gray wool of cocoons. Gray, gray like God, nothing in there

but sleep. But then something quivered ever so slightly, something all wrinkled up and folded on itself like scrunched up
paper. It gave the faintest little shiver, it fluttered like it
could almost breathe. Slowly it opened and spread itself
out. A color like melted caramel spread along the edges of
its wings, and in the soft, powdery lavender dust, four eyes
opened in the middle, as empty-dark as the eyes of my father's angel, all radiance and majesty just like my father
said. I could see the feelers poke out, all feathery and trem-
bling in the sunlight. Then her furry brown body started
pumping up and down laying piles of ivory colored eggs just
like my father said she would, each one tinier than the head
on my mother's tacking pins.

The air outside made me shiver. I closed the box
tight so she couldn't fly away. Flies came whining close to
the curtains, buzzing around in the sunlight, looking for
something nasty to sit on. Outside I could hear all the sparrows arguing on the roof, but my butterfly was safe in her
cake box and they couldn't get to her. I went back to bed,
but I had to get up one more time because I forgot to leave
her box open a crack so my butterfly could get air.

I missed Madame D'Eau, and I missed Snow White even
more. And I kept wishing I could go downstairs so I could
play with Walter, but the doctor told my mother I had to
stay in bed. My mother got me this box with all different
colors in it. You could fit all the crayons in their little paper
cradles and line them up inside just like colored lollipops,
only there were five purple flavors at least, and four different kinds of blues, and so many greens you almost couldn't

tell where one green stopped and another green started. But purple was my favorite. And magenta. And fuschia. And aquamarine.

I kept asking my mother when I could get up, but I didn't think it was a good idea to let on about how I wanted to play with Walter, so I just said how I wanted to go out. Every day, I would tiptoe to the window where I could prop the lid of her cake box open so I could watch my butterfly lay eggs. I didn't know what to call her, maybe Radiance, except it sounded like Prudence, so I named her Majesty, just like my father's angel. Except when my father came to see me, he said she wasn't a butterfly at all, she really was a moth and you could tell because she had feathers on her feelers. He said she was a cecropia, but I just called her Majesty.

Majesty kept laying eggs. She didn't care if I flushed them down the toilet as fast as they piled up. She went on laying them anyway, except her body was starting to get flat. I could tell she must be hungry but she didn't like the leaf I broke off from my hyacinth to feed her. Maybe it tasted like carrots to her. She just kept laying eggs and getting flatter, and her wings got all ratty the way flowers get before people have to throw them out. I wished I could find her a leaf from the kind of tree she was hanging on when I picked her off the branch. My father said it was a sycamore.

I didn't tell my mother I had to find a sycamore because my mother didn't like Majesty. She said she was dirty and she didn't want her laying eggs all over the house. I kept asking my mother when I could get out of bed, but she said I had to wait. That's when I got the idea to tell her I had an important message I had to give to Joe so could I please go out.

"Joe doesn't run the elevator anymore."

"How come?"

"He went away."

I got this drumming feeling in my stomach. I couldn't tell what it was. When I asked my mother where he went to, she said she didn't know. I asked her why did he have to go. She said how Joe had this bottle with milk in it for Walter, only he got into a fight with Mr. Kepke and he hit Mr. Kepke with a bottle. That's how come I found out what happened that day I saw Mr. Kepke bleeding and cursing down in the basement corridor. I didn't want my mother to know I had a secret, but I couldn't help asking her anyhow. "Why did he get into a fight?"

"Because Mr. Kepke didn't like Walter because he was always making messes everywhere and Mr. Kepke didn't want him inside the house. He wanted Joe to get rid of him."

I got scared that maybe Joe ran down the stairs with Walter wiggling under his arm like that because he was going to get rid of him. I remembered what my mother said that time about Snow White.

"Did he have to put Walter to sleep?"

My mother said she didn't know, but the drumming in my stomach wouldn't go away.

One time when I was sitting up, my mother put a book on my bed. It had a paper cover on it with colored pictures of raindrops falling everywhere. I asked my mother where it came from. She said Madame D'Eau gave it to her when she went to visit her in the nursing home. It even had her name on it: *L'histoire d'une Goutte D'Eau.* My mother said it was the story of a drop of water, and Madame D'Eau gave it to her as a present for me. She let me look at the pictures. She sat on the bed so she could read it to me and every time she was done, she let me turn the page.

First there was a rainstorm, more like a thunder storm, and you could see all the colored slashes where the raindrops were supposed to be coming down. But this one little raindrop didn't land on a flower or a leaf like all the other little raindrops did. She fell into a little stream with rocks in it and waterfalls, and the sky turned all pink after she came down, and she got swept along till she got to a creek where the woodcutters were floating logs, and she went into a canal where a bargeman talked to her, and she got swept along in the big river past Lyon, where my mother said Madame D'Eau was born. And on she swept to the great ocean where she saw fishing boats and ocean liners and then she disappeared. That was the end of the story, and when my mother let me turn it, there was a rainbow on the very last page.

"How come it has a rainbow? Because it stopped raining and the sun came out?"

My mother just nodded, but she didn't say anything.

Every time my mother let me get out of bed, she said how thin I got but I felt hungry all the time. I kept asking her to cook me a chicken, the kind she used to stuff with bread. Maybe if she had to go to the butcher, she could take me with her because that's where the sycamores were growing with the leaves that Majesty liked best. But when my mother got ready to go, she said I couldn't come with her yet because I wasn't strong enough.

I waited till I could hear her footsteps disappearing down the hall. When I heard the elevator go down, I unbuttoned my pajamas and threw them under the bed. I got on my underwear and stuck my arms inside my dress. I got into my leggings and put on my coat and hat. I didn't even bother with my shoes because I was in a hurry. I just kicked them under the bed with my pajamas and put on my galoshes. I got Majesty's cake box off the window sill.

I didn't even ring for the elevator in case my mother forgot something and had to come back upstairs. I went all the way down the stairs, the same stairs we had to go up, Joe and me, the day I got to play with Walter, but I had to go one at a time because my galoshes kept trying to come off and the cake box kept getting in the way so I couldn't see the stairs. When I ran through the lobby, my galoshes went clompclompclomp, but I didn't care because the lobby was empty and nobody could see. I went running down the hill and around the corner. I was panting and puffing. I was trying to go even faster but my galoshes kept falling off. If I could just cross the big avenue and get to the other side where the sycamores were growing. I was trying to go faster, but my galoshes kept coming off.

A white dog was coming my way, running very fast, a big white dog with a little black spot over one eye. It was Walter! Walter, all grown up almost, with his very own leash. It was just a clothes line, but Joe was holding the other end of it. And he said, "Hi, sugar!" and everything came running up on me at once, how I wished Joe could still be our elevator man, how I really missed him, and if he was going to get to keep Walter now he didn't have to work for Mr. Kepke anymore, and how come he didn't go to jail for getting in a fight, but then maybe it wouldn't be good to let on what my mother told me, so I just said how he was and how

I was sorry he couldn't be our elevator man.

"We O.K., sugar, me and Walter. We jus' fine."

Then he said how I was. I wished I could tell him all about how I had new monia and the bed kept whooshing upside down and how I was so sick I even had to drink from a baby bottle just like Walter did, but I was scared my mother would come back even though I fixed the little buttons on the door so I wouldn't have to ring. So I asked him if maybe he could just cross me to the other side to where the sycamores were growing.

"What you want with sycamores?"

"So Majesty can eat." And I lifted the lid and showed him Majesty sitting all starving and ratty-looking in her box. I asked if he could please cross me over and wait for me while I got Majesty some leaves.

"Sure, sugar, jus' hold onto my hand." We had to wait for traffic for a long time before it got safe to cross. I kept worrying my mother would come back. When we got to the other side, Joe let go my hand. "Take yo' time, sister. We be waiting right here to cross you back, me and Walter. He need time to do his business."

I was trying to run just as fast as my galoshes let me, down, down the gravel path to where the sycamores were growing. You could see the first green shoots poking out and that kind of spotty bark they have that looks like old paint peeling all the time, and all the fuzzy little pompons left over from the winter, still hanging from their branches, and all the pigeons waddling their rainbow necks and cooing and bowing and turning around and sweeping their tail feathers along the ground, ocurotokee, ocurotokee.

I climbed up on the bench. I stood on tippytoes and stretched and stretched, but I couldn't even reach the lowest branch. Even if my father was there for me to climb up on his shoulders, it was still too high for even someone big to reach. I couldn't tell what to do because I had to get back before my mother did. But then I thought maybe if I left Majesty there she could find the sycamores herself.

I saw this little clump of bushes just a little farther on. I had to put my arm clear around Majesty's box to protect her from the snapping branches so I could crawl inside.

"Don't be scared," I said to her. I stuck my hand inside her box. I could feel her crawling up my finger, tickling me, first one foot and then another. I made a bridge for her so she could get up on a branch deep inside the thicket where the sparrows couldn't get her. One leg and then another. I waited till she got all her feet up on the branch. I could see the big eyes staring out of the middle of her wings, as empty-dark as my father's angel, and even all tattered, she still looked beautiful.

I watched her take her first shaky step. She nearly lost her balance, but I stuck my finger out again to help her get back on. She just stayed there very still. She didn't move or anything, except I could see her breathing.

ABOUT THE AUTHOR

Cecile Pineda was born in Harlem. She grew up in an apartment house in New York City. Pineda has always been fascinated by insects, including moths, ants, termites, not to mention cockroaches. Her published novels include *The Love Queen of the Amazon*, written with the support of a NEA Fiction Fellowship, and named Notable Book of the Year by the New York Times, *Frieze*, set in Ninth Century India and Java; and *Face*, which was nominated for an American Book Award. *Face* received the Gold Medal from the Commonwealth Club of California, and the Sue Kaufman Prize given by the American Academy and Institute of Arts & Letters. Pineda has completed two mononovels, *Redoubt*, a meditation on gender, and *BARDO99*, which presents the 20th Century as a character. Both *Redoubt* and *BARDO99* will be published by Wings Press in the near future, along with new editions of her earlier novels. Pineda teaches creative writing in the San Francisco-Bay Area.

For more information on Cecile Pineda, visit her webpage at http://www.home.earthlink.net/~cecilep

Colophon

Two thousand copies of *Fishlight: A Dream of Childhood*, by Cecile Pineda, have been printed on 70 pound natural linen paper, containing fifty percent recycled fiber, by Williams Printing & Graphics of San Antonio, Texas. The first one hundred copies of *Fishlight* were numbered, signed, and dated by the author. Five hundred copies were bound as hardbacks. Text and titles were set in a contemporary version of Classic Bodoni. The font was originally designed by 18th century Italian punchcutter and typographer, Giambattista Bodoni, press director for the Duke of Parma. *Fishlight* was entirely designed and produced by Bryce Milligan, publisher, Wings Press.

Wings Press was founded in 1975 by J. Whitebird and Joseph F. Lomax as "an informal association of artists and cultural mythologists dedicated to the preservation of the literature of the nation of Texas." The publisher/editor since 1995, Bryce Milligan is honored to carry on and expand that mission to include the finest in American writing.

Recent and forthcoming titles from Wings Press

Way of Whiteness by Wendy Barker (2000)

Burnt Water Suite by Darrell Bourque (1999)

Hook & Bloodline by Chip Dameron (2000)

Splintered Silences by Greta de León (2000)

Incognito by María Espinosa (Spring 2002)

Peace in the Corazón by Victoria García-Zapata (1999)

Street of the Seven Angels by John Howard Griffin (Fall 2001)

Cande, te estoy llamando by Celeste Guzmán (1999)

Winter Poems from Eagle Pond by Donald Hall (1999)

Initiations in the Abyss by Jim Harter (Fall 2001)

Strong Box Heart by Sheila Sánchez Hatch (2000)

Seven Cigarette Story by Courtenay Martin (1999)

Fishlight: A Dream of Childhood by Cecile Pineda (Fall 2001)

The Love Queen of the Amazon by Cecile Pineda (Fall 2001)

Mama Yetta and Other Poems by Hermine Pinson (1999)

Smolt by Nicole Pollentier (1999)

Long Story Short by Mary Grace Rodríguez (1999)

Garabato Poems by Virgil Suárez (1999)

Sonnets to Human Beings by Carmen Tafolla (1999)

Sonnets and Salsa by Carmen Tafolla (Spring 2001))

The Laughter of Doves by Frances Marie Treviño (Fall 2001)

Finding Peaches in the Desert by Pam Uschuk (2000)

Vida by Alma Luz Villanueva (Fall 2001)